I Do

A.J. PINE

Entangled Publishing, LLC
2614 South Timberline Road
Suite 109
Fort Collins, CO 80525
Visit our website at www.entangledpublishing.com.

Embrace is an imprint of Entangled Publishing, LLC.

Edited by Karen Grove
Cover design by Heather Howland
Cover art from iStock

Manufactured in the United States of America

First Edition November 2015

embrace

For my family. I do *love you.*

Chapter One

JORDAN

There is no such thing as overpacking. There is no such thing as overpacking. There is no such thing as overpacking.

Now all Jordan had to do was click her heels together three times and her suitcase would close, right?

"Finished!" Noah yelled from the kitchen/living room—the *only* other room aside from the bedroom and a sad excuse for a bathroom.

"Packing or grading?" Jordan asked before dropping down, butt first, onto the unzipped case. She blew a lock of hair out of her eyes, but it fell back as soon as the puff of air left her lips.

"Figures," she mumbled. She couldn't even contain her hair. How would she contain the contents necessary for a trip overseas where she would be a bridesmaid for the first time? She didn't know how to bridesmaid, let alone perform such duties in a foreign country. So she packed everything from a bathing suit to a parka. Maybe one of the two would have to go.

She looked up, sensing Noah's presence, expecting quiet condescension at her inability to embrace the whole *less is more* concept.

Instead, he leaned in the doorframe and quirked a brow, dark waves flopping over his forehead.

"Both." His brows furrowed. "I finished both. Grading and packing." Noah's eyes drank her in. "Nice outfit, Brooks." The left corner of his mouth hinted at a grin. Then he was squatting in front of her, lifting the strap of her camisole that had strayed from her shoulder.

Goose bumps peppered Jordan's skin at the soft graze of his fingertips. God, he could still set her on fire with the simplest touch, even after three years.

"I mean it," he continued, his lips trailing after his fingers, brushing her pebbled skin. "This is my favorite outfit of yours. You should wear it every day."

Butterflies danced in her belly at the low rasp of his voice. He dropped to his knees, resting a hand on her bare thigh and using the other to free her neck from its blanket of hair.

He nipped at the flesh below her ear, and she let out something between a sigh and a moan.

"This *is* what I wear every day...unless I'm in class." She tried to sound annoyed, to assure the beautiful man doing beautiful things to her that she *would* wear more than pajamas at home—once grad school was over and she was done volleying between her own writing projects and grading those of her undergrad students.

"Do you remember what I look like in real clothes? Because I don't. I'm not even sure I can wear a dress to the wedding. My body may actually reject it, like a virus." She flailed her arms and added, "Danger, Will Robinson. Foreign object. Must destroy."

This didn't deter him. Jordan was ready to protest further,

but then Noah's fingertips reached the hem of her boy shorts, and she forgot why she was so frustrated. That is, until Noah's lips found hers, and the two of them lost their balance, tumbling over the side of the *still* unzipped suitcase and into the frame of their bed.

"Shit!" she said.

Jordan rubbed her temple, and Noah massaged his shoulder.

He chuckled. "Loving you really is a contact sport, isn't it?" He kissed the spot where her head had greeted the metal frame. "You okay?"

Jordan sighed. "You still love me? You do see the mess sitting in front of you, right?"

"Technically," he said, his grin widening, "you're more sprawled than sitting."

She reached over her head to grab a pillow, but Noah caught her wrist before she could whack him with it. This was good, the two of them finding a few moments to pretend like all they had on their list was getting her suitcase closed. It wasn't that things weren't good between them. They were perfect when they had time for little moments like this. But the whole being-an-adult thing—classes, teaching, the day-to-day stresses—often got in the way.

"You're so busy," she said. "We both are. And…" Her voice broke a bit on that word, so she cleared her throat and tried to hold it together. "I feel like everything around us is so crazy. I just…I miss you."

It sounded silly saying that when he was next to her in bed every night. But it was the truth. She thought back to the year they'd met studying abroad in Scotland, how it took them ten months to finally get things right. Despite how difficult the whole falling-in-love thing was, it seemed like a cakewalk compared to balancing her MFA with Noah's first years as a teacher. They just needed a small window of *simple*. A reboot.

She wanted to remind him that someday it would be more like this—quiet time alone instead of the tornado that had been their lives for the past three years—maybe even with less physical injury.

"Your suitcase?" he said. "That's a mess. But you, Brooks?" He pulled her to him, scooping her up and depositing her onto his lap. "I'm so proud of you. You thought you had no direction when we met, and look at you now. You're a student, a teacher, and soon your passion for writing will also be your career." He kissed her softly on the forehead. "You amaze me. Every single day."

Jordan took in a sharp breath. Yes, his touch could still drive her crazy, but it was the things he said—ridiculous things like being proud of her when she still felt so directionless—that melted her heart.

"And I miss you, too," he said, his voice growing serious so she knew she wasn't imagining the strain. "We'll get through this—the hard stuff. And God, *yes*, I love you. Never question that."

She kissed him, teasing his bottom lip with her tongue and teeth as she felt his smile against hers. They would get past the hard part, wouldn't they?

"Run away with me to Greece," she whispered to him.

"Already got my passport," he answered, warm breath mingling with her own.

"And your kilt?"

Noah's smile widened, and she leaned back to see his blue eyes shine at her.

"*And* my kilt," he said.

With that he snuck a finger under the hem he'd teased before.

"We still have an hour before the taxi comes." His statement came out like a question.

"How long will it take you to fix my suitcase problem?"

Jordan asked.

He lay her back gently on the floor, one finger still under the soft cotton, tracing the line where her thigh connected to her hip—following it down until Jordan wasn't sure she'd even bring a suitcase anymore, not if ditching the wardrobe meant more time for Noah to torment her until she forgot her own name.

His thumb brushed over the outside of her shorts, right between her legs, and yep—she might as well have been nameless at that point. But when he whispered *Brooks*, she knew without a doubt who she was.

She was the girl who fell for the boy and somehow managed to make it work for three years and counting. He was now the man she always knew he'd become, and together they were headed back to where it all began—to watch her former roommate, Elaina, and the boy in the kilt she swore she'd never fall for, Duncan, say, "I do." Then Jordan and Noah would trace their steps back to Scotland, where they'd met and where they'd gotten it all so wrong before finally getting it right.

"Screw the suitcase," she whispered, and Noah's lips traced the line of her jaw until they rested at her ear.

"As you wish."

NOAH

Jordan strode past the skycap, and Noah followed her into the terminal.

"We could have checked the bags outside," he told her. He may have purged half her closet from her luggage, but that didn't mean he wanted to weave through an amusement park–length line with both their bags when they could have taken care of it outside.

Once in line, she turned to face him.

"This way we save a little extra cash."

She combed the hair off his brow, and, well, he couldn't argue with the logic of her touch—or the fact that this trip was already costing them money they didn't have. But for the next week, he didn't want her to worry about money or graduation or any of the normal, daily stressors.

He waggled his brows. "Means I can buy some shitty airplane headphones for the in-flight entertainment."

Jordan hooked a finger in the collar of his T-shirt.

"I thought I was your in-flight entertainment." She pouted, and Noah's pants suddenly grew tighter in the groin region.

"Jesus, Brooks. We're not even checked in yet."

She bit her lip, then unbuttoned her gray peacoat and unwound her scarf. Her V-neck T-shirt was pulled off center so he could see the strap of her bra. The short flight from Columbus to New York meant not much more than an hour of alone time before meeting up with the rest of the group, and then plenty of time for his pants to loosen up on their own.

Noah sighed.

"What?" Jordan asked, but her grin told him she knew what she did to him.

"Did you really seat us next to…"

For fuck's sake. He sounded like enough of a dick without finishing the question, but the words were already out there. God, he hated Jordan seeing him like this.

"Griffin and Maggie?" Of course she finished the thought. "No, we're not next to them. We're one row in front of them. And, babe? It's been three years. We're past all that, right?"

The line was moving now, which gave him a reprieve from having to look her in the eye and tell her that yes, when he wasn't thinking about how he almost blew his chance with her three years ago, he was past *all that*, past her dating Griffin when Noah said they could only be friends despite how much he knew he was falling for her. But when *all that* was going to be sitting one row behind them for eleven and a half hours and spending the weekend with them, it was hard not to go back there in his head.

When Jordan hefted her suitcase onto the scale at the check-in counter, Noah gave his messenger bag, still slung over his shoulder, a safety pat, reassuring himself of the small velvet box inside. He would have a do-over after their time in Greece, on the train ride from London to Scotland. As long as everything went according to plan—no unnecessary stress for the girl who never relaxed—he would leave the States with his girlfriend and return with his fiancée.

Jordan gasped, patted her pockets, riffled through her purse, and Noah's eyes grew wide.

"My passport!" she yelled. "Shit, Noah, my passport!"

He let out a long, shaky breath as he pulled *both* their passports from the back pocket of his jeans and lay them down on the counter.

Nervous laughter erupted from his girlfriend's lips.

"This trip is going to be the end of me, isn't it?" she asked as she steadied herself against the counter.

He looped his arm around her waist and drew her near as the airline attendant checked their bags to New York and through their connecting flight to Thessaloniki, Greece.

No, he hoped. *This is only the beginning.*

Chapter Two

G riffin stared at the envelope on the counter. The envelope…stared back.

Chickenshit, it said. He could hear the stupid thing judging him.

He ran a hand through his hair and laughed.

"It's a freaking envelope," he said to himself. "You open the mail every day." Yet he still hadn't touched the taunting piece of paper.

And with that, he ignored the thumping of his heart and the dampness of his palms, tearing it open before he could chicken out again.

Because he was a man of logic, Griffin held his breath as he began to read, deciding that nothing was real or official until he exhaled.

Dear Mr. Reed,
Congratulations. We are pleased to inform you that out

of hundreds of applicants, you have been chosen for the AmeriCorps Eli Segal Fellowship...

Griffin exhaled. He was sure there was more written on the document, but all his mind kept looping on replay was *Congratulations.*

This had been nothing more than a whim, applying for the fellowship. The same as ditching his father's job offer and joining AmeriCorps. Now he had two whims adding up to major life changes, which should be great. It would be damn near perfect if he hadn't neglected to tell Maggie he was doing it. But what were the chances of him winning the fellowship when only *one* person got it a year? It wasn't worth planting the seed of moving to D.C. when the odds were so not in his favor.

...After the terms of your current AmeriCorps post are served, we welcome you to Washington, D.C., for your thirteen-month position as the next Eli Segal fellow. We expect your confirmation of acceptance no later than January 14th. Congratulations on entering the next phase in your country's national service. We look forward to seeing you in Washington.

Excellent. Two weeks to make a decision that would affect not one life...but two. And a trip to another country in between. No pressure.

The apartment door flew open, and he acted on instinct, hurriedly folding the paper and shoving it in his back pocket as Maggie beelined for the bathroom.

Shit.

She knelt over the toilet and heaved, and in seconds Griffin was there with what he knew she needed: her emergency migraine medication injection.

"Hey, Pippi," he said, his voice gentle as she collapsed

on her butt against the shower door. Tears streaked her face as Griffin pushed a tangerine wave behind her ear. "I got ya, sweetheart," and he held up the syringe for her to see.

Maggie nodded as he slid her long skirt up over her knee, rested the syringe atop her bare thigh, and pressed the button. He still winced when he had to do it, but Maggie didn't even flinch. She was a pro…or more likely in too much pain to register the needle piercing her skin. She was now a three-year survivor of a brain aneurysm. Griffin hated that days like today would forever be a part of Maggie's life, yet he admired her acceptance. Her strength. She had to live her life differently than she did a few years ago, dealing with chronic headaches and short-term memory loss, but she was no longer living in fear of *What if?* He just thanked his lucky stars he was home to be here when she needed him.

He stood to wet a washcloth with cold water, then dropped down next to his girl, putting an arm around her and leaning her head on his shoulder.

"How's this?" he asked, his voice soft and low as he rested the cloth on her forehead. She closed her eyes, even though the light was off, and forced a small smile through the pain and nodded.

This wasn't the norm, but it also wasn't a surprise. Maggie had had a final exam this morning, an art presentation this afternoon, and then worked a shift at Royal Grounds. To accommodate her first year back with a full class load, two professors allowed her to finish her final projects during the holiday break. But sometimes too much was just too much, especially with her health history. So he held her and waited for the medicine to take effect. Fifteen or twenty minutes usually did the trick, and as much as he hated seeing her like this, he always appreciated a few quiet minutes with Maggie in his arms.

"Thank you, Fancy Pants."

Griffin stirred, apparently having dozed—lulled by her breathing and the crash from the adrenaline rush of the letter and Maggie's entrance.

"Look who's back," he teased, and then kissed the top of her head.

"Don't let your lips go any farther than that," she said as she maneuvered out of his arms and stood. "I need to brush my teeth, do the whole post-migraine cleanup."

She smiled weakly, and Griffin joined her where she stood.

"You need to lie down," he said. That was the drill. Migraine, meds, nap. Then she would be good as new.

"I need to shower," she insisted.

He raised a brow. "I can help you with that." The corners of his mouth turned up. But he was only teasing, expecting her to say *no* regardless of how much he'd love to be with her. Griffin always felt the need to reassure her in these moments, to show her that her health—any small setbacks—didn't scare him.

Maggie turned on the sink and splashed cold water on her face. Then she loaded her toothbrush with a decent helping of paste, and then pointed the toothbrush at him.

"Start the water, and make it hot, please. I want to burn away this day."

Griffin obliged while Maggie started to brush.

"That bad, huh?" he asked.

She held up a finger as she finished her routine, which always ended with a minute-long mouthwash finale.

"The school stuff was okay," she said. "Just draining. I mean, I couldn't have studied more for that final, you know? But the coffee house was nuts. And Miles took the night off to work on his dissertation, and…" She let out a long breath and looped her arms around Griffin's waist. "And I'm just glad to be home with you, where everything is quiet, and normal, and

I can finally breathe."

Griffin swallowed hard, feeling the folded piece of paper burning a hole in his pocket—singeing Maggie's need for normal. Tonight was not the night to shake up her world. Instead he dipped his head toward hers, letting his lips brush her minty fresh mouth. She responded, her lips parting and inviting his tongue to mingle with hers.

Maggie's hands left his waist, making their way to the button of his jeans. Maybe he was thinking about this shaking-up-her-world thing all wrong.

"Are you sure?" he asked, not able to mask the hoarseness of his voice.

She unfastened the button and tugged down his zipper, resting her palm on his erection. He hissed, bracing himself against the shower door as steam enveloped them.

She kissed him hard, hand gripping him with the same intensity.

"After today?" She kissed him again. "There's nothing I want more." She laughed quietly. "This and then sleep. *Lots* of sleep."

She helped him out of his jeans, her eyes darting to the floor as she saw the letter tumble from his pocket as the pants fell from his hips.

"What's that?" she asked, and Griffin's eyes met hers. He lifted her Royal Grounds T-shirt over her head, loving the way she raised her arms to let him do it.

"God, you're beautiful. Do you know that?"

She bit her lip as she smiled.

He drank in the vision before him, ginger waves resting against her freckle-dotted alabaster skin. The weariness in her eyes did nothing to mask the soul-deep beauty they always held when they looked at him. She was really his, and Griffin still couldn't believe it. He would do nothing to fuck this up, even if it meant closing the door on Washington. He didn't need the fellowship, hadn't even thought he'd get it. But he needed Maggie. That went without question.

He kicked his jeans and the letter out of the way.

"It's nothing," he told her, almost believing the lie as he unclasped her bra and covered her breasts with his hands. "But you, Pippi? You're everything."

Chapter Three

"This was a mistake." Miles paced as he watched Jordan and Noah approach the gate. "I have never felt like a third wheel with you guys, but I'm a fifth wheel now. Why did I let you talk me into this?"

He was on his way to Europe for a wedding, which had sounded great when Maggie made him the offer. He was long overdue for a vacation, and he certainly didn't want to shirk his best-friend duties, but now he wasn't so sure. He didn't even know Duncan and Elaina. Had never met them. And now here he was, off to what would be a romantic weekend for the happy couple, for Maggie and Griffin, and for their friends Jordan and Noah—two more people he'd never met, by the way. Romantic weekends away really weren't Miles's thing, especially when he was flying solo.

Commitment. The thought gave him the shakes. And now he'd be surrounded by it for three days. Seventy-two hours of people oohing and ahhing and blotting their tears because the happy couple was just so damned…happy

Maggie hooked her arm in his as his pacing brought him back in her direction, walking with him now toward the Hudson News across from the gate's seating area. "Because, sweetie. Technically, I need a plus-one. Griffin's doing all that best-man stuff, and with Jordan and Noah in the wedding, too, who's going to hang with little ol' me?"

Miles stopped to face her just as they entered the shop, his whole demeanor softening when he looked at his best friend. Maggie's smile was tentative, and the last thing he wanted to do was ruin this trip for her. She was nervous enough as it was, this trip putting a twist into her carefully constructed schedule.

He smiled back and watched her shoulders relax.

"I'm sorry," he said. "You know I would do anything for you, and I'm happy to do this. It's just—"

Maggie interrupted. "You miss Paige."

Miles sighed. She was half right. Although things had gotten more serious with his most recent ex than he'd ever expected—and while it did kind of suck that she moved to California—he was more relieved than anything else. Miles missed having someone to talk to at the end of a long shift. He missed the regularity of someone in his bed. But he'd never been one to set down roots, so yeah, Paige planting hers across the country saved him from having to deal with that.

"Sure, I miss her," he said, thumbing through the paperbacks on an endcap.

"*Mi*-iles…"

Shit. He knew Maggie was onto him when she did that two-syllable thing with his name.

"Mags?" He kept his eyes on the half-naked couple posing on the cover of a book.

"Spill it, darlin'. Something's up, or else we wouldn't be hiding out in the gift shop when I'm dying to introduce you to

Jordan and Noah."

She pulled the book from his hands and placed it firmly back on the shelf. He groaned and faced her.

"I don't do weddings, Mags. I mean, I'm happy to do anything for you, but as a general rule I've got a pretty firm negative on the whole watching-two-people-pledge-their-lives-to-each-other thing."

She rolled her eyes. "God, Miles. I thought this thing with Paige was going to suck some of that cynicism out of you, but I guess I was wrong."

He cupped her face in his palms.

"Sorry, honey. Still filled to the brim."

She backed away, crossing her arms over her chest.

"What if…what if when you and I…" She pointed back and forth between them. "Wow. I'm glad we didn't work out. I'd have just been another notch on your bedpost."

Whoa, whoa, *whoa*. How did letting a little bit of honesty through turn into Maggie being pissed at him? Miles crossed his arms right back at her, narrowing his eyes.

"You didn't," he started and waited for her to object, but she said nothing. "You didn't fall for me, Mags, because you *knew* you wouldn't, just like I knew I wouldn't fall for you."

"But…"

He didn't let her finish.

"But nothing. It was *safe*—for both of us. That's why we let it happen, and that's why we never let it go any further. We love each other too much to mess with a good thing."

Maggie's shoulders sagged, and he knew he'd won, but that didn't stop the twist of guilt in his gut. He didn't want to deflate her spirit just to prove a point, but he also knew he played by different rules than she did. Maggie was a hopeless romantic at heart. It just took meeting Griffin to get her to step out of her safe zone. Miles had stepped out of the safe zone years ago, and all it did was teach him that loving someone wasn't enough, not in his experience. He hoped it worked for Maggie. He'd never seen her happier, and he actually liked Griffin, who got how special Maggie was. He wasn't against kicking the former rich boy's ass if he hurt his best friend, but if there was one couple Miles was rooting for, it was them.

"You know what?" she asked, grabbing his hand and squeezing it in hers. "Playing it safe? It wasn't living. *You're* the one who told me that." She rested a hand on his chest, the left side, just over his heart. "I know everything about you, Miles. Everything except for who messed you up so much in here."

He cleared his throat, plastered on one of his patented grins, and pulled her out of the shop.

"I'm the psych PhD candidate, honey. Not you. Not everyone has some big story of heartbreak to psychoanalyze. Some of us simply like all play and no work. How about you let me be that guy?"

He led her toward the gate, the taste of the lie sour on his tongue. Safe meant never again having to explain away his partner's unfounded jealousy in relation to his bisexuality. Safe meant enjoying another's company without fear of attachment. Safe meant never giving your heart to another just so that person could use it up, suck the soul from it, and return nothing but the shell of what it used to be.

Maybe safe wasn't truly living, but Miles had been doing it for so long he'd forgotten what living felt like anyway.

They crossed the short distance back to the gate where Griffin now sat with two gorgeous brunettes—one female and one male—both smiling at his and Maggie's approach.

Maggie squeezed his hand again.

"Okay," she said. "I'll let you be that guy…for now. For this trip. Because that's what the next few days are all about. Fun. *Play*. But this conversation isn't over."

"Noted," he said quietly as they came into earshot of

their traveling companions. He'd take this short reprieve, and maybe when they got back, he'd tell her about Cole, the only secret he'd ever kept from her. Right now he plastered that grin in place and continued with the Miles Show everyone seemed to adore.

He dropped Maggie's hand and held it out toward the new members of the group who, along with Griffin, stood on their approach.

"You must be Noah," he said, and Noah nodded as he shook Miles's hand.

"Guess that makes you Miles," he said.

Miles turned toward the woman to Noah's right and bent to kiss her on the cheek. "The lovely Jordan Brooks I've heard so much about."

Jordan's cheeks flushed pink, and he watched the slight twitch of muscle in Noah's jaw as Griffin's eyes darted to the floor.

That, he thought. *That's what I'll never have to worry about again. Jealousy. Trust.* Miles had his heart broken once because of both, and once was enough to know he wasn't putting himself out there again. Here was the proof, two happy couples who still let that shit get in the way. It was poison. He knew how much Griffin loved Maggie and was certain Noah felt the same for Jordan. But three years hadn't erased the tension between the two guys who once loved the same girl. And three years certainly hadn't erased Miles's memory of how it felt to constantly reassure Cole that he loved only him, that he didn't want to fuck every beautiful man or woman who he passed on the street. Gay, straight, bi—none of that shit ever mattered to Miles. He didn't do labels. He had just always followed his heart. But Cole didn't get it. He thought being true to his heart meant Miles could never truly be faithful. Miles *never* cheated, but the one man he loved assumed he would. Miles had always been proud of who he was. Only now he was proud with a dash of bitter and a pinch of fear. He hated Cole for doing that to him. But at least it protected him from getting hurt again. That was the trade-off.

He'd smile for Maggie…and for the rest of the crew, but inside he was bah-humbugging the shit out of his current situation.

"It's nice to meet you," he said, just as the announcement came that boarding for Thessaloniki was about to begin. "Shall we get this party started?"

Chapter Four

*E*laina McAllister.

The first time she'd kissed Duncan—on his birthday more than three years ago—Elaina Tripoli had said the name to herself. *Silently*, of course, because admitting to such a thought would have meant betraying her trademark Greek stoicism, and lovesick puppy she was not. At least not in public.

Never mind that the boy in the skirt, the Scotsman who *never* hid how he felt, probably didn't remember that first kiss, thanks to enough whisky and pints to sedate a highland bull.

But Elaina hadn't forgotten, not the kiss nor the sound of her future name echoing between her ears, the name that would be hers before tomorrow was done.

"Elaina, *eísai xýpnios*?"

The door swung open before Elaina had a chance to reveal that she was, in fact, awake.

She rolled her eyes. "*Eláte se*, Theodora."

Come in.

Thea waved a hand in her cousin's face and pushed her down in the chair in front of the vanity.

"Look at you, *exádelfos.* You didn't sleep last night?"

Thea swiped a thumb under Elaina's eye, proving the purple tint to her skin had nothing to do with smudged makeup.

Elaina huffed. "Everyone is supposed to speak English today...tomorrow. The McAllister family does not know Greek."

Again with the waving, as if Elaina were an annoying mosquito Thea merely had to swat out of the way rather than a bride-to-be who didn't need reminding about the bags under her eyes.

"*Exádelfos.* Cousin. Why does this matter when the McAllisters aren't in the room?"

Elaina's face broke into a smile that surprised even her.

Thea looked her up and down. "You have gone soft, Elaina."

On instinct, Elaina's hand wrapped around her torso, and her stomach muscles contracted. It was her father's fault, really. His and his assistant chef's. They always made too much food, but that was what happened when your father owned a restaurant. And when they left her all the extras in the refrigerator, well? A belly was bound to go a little soft.

You need to sample, Elaina. Taste before the guests do. Make sure everything is nóstima.

"Not soft *there*," Thea said, pointing to Elaina's belly. "*Here.*" Thea's finger rested above Elaina's heart, and the bride-to-be couldn't contain her grin.

Elaina sighed. "You are right. But if you tell him, I will hunt you down and kill you."

Her cousin laughed. "Your secret is safe with me. All the world will still fear you; only I will know you have a marshmallow heart."

Elaina's eyes narrowed at Thea, but she had lost the battle—if there ever was one. Duncan was so much more than she'd ever expected. He was everything she never knew she wanted, and now he was on his way to Greece. To marry her. And leave his home for hers.

As Thea opened her makeup bag to begin work on her cousin's almost-married face, something caught in Elaina's throat, and she tried to swallow it back down.

"What?" Thea asked, makeup brush poised to sweep powder across Elaina's nose.

"It is nothing," Elaina said, with all the conviction of a child swallowing a spoonful of medicine.

Thea dropped to the bed next to her chair and let the powder brush fall to her lap.

"What?" she asked again, making it clear that she was not going to help Elaina get ready for the pre-wedding celebration until she spilled her always-guarded thoughts.

Elaina looked down, an attempt to hide the first tear that fell. Thea's hand covered hers, and she decided it was time to let it all out.

"He's giving up so much," Elaina said.

"Your papa gave him a good job managing the restaurant," Thea countered.

"He is leaving his home."

"For a new one with you." This time Thea squeezed Elaina's hand, eliciting a weak smile from her. "Come. Let's get you ready. Papa already left to pick up the McAllisters. He does not want them eating hotel food, so he has *galatopita* waiting downstairs in the restaurant's private room. When does Duncan's plane land?"

Elaina swiped a finger under each eye, collecting herself to greet her guests—her new family. This might be the room she grew up in, part of the apartment over the restaurant she shared with her parents and grandmother, but today it felt foreign. New. Tonight would be the last night she slept in the bed on which Thea sat, the one meant only for *her*. Tomorrow would be the hotel suite, and after the honeymoon, the new apartment she'd share with Duncan. Her husband.

Elaina's phone sat on the table in front of her, and she woke the screen and saw she'd missed a text message.

Her eyes grew wide, and she beamed as she held the phone up for Thea to see. No need to worry about travel plans when she had all of Duncan's information at her fingertips.

Thea shook her head and pursed her lips. "Please explain this text," she said, squinting at the screen. "Flight 2342 from Athens to Thessaloniki: Landed. Seat 17D: Vacant."

Elaina rolled her eyes. Did she have to spell it out for her cousin?

"It is an app for the phone." Thea raised a brow. "Yes, I know how to use my phone. It is an app with Duncan's flight information, and it gives me all the updates on his trip. See? It says his plane has landed and that his seat is…"

Elaina looked at the phone again. She scrolled through earlier notifications from Duncan's flight from England to Athens.

Flight 2091 from England to Athens: Landed. Seat 23B: Occupied.

"He didn't get on the second plane," she said, her voice flat. Then a sense of panic kicked in. "What if something happened to him?"

Thea put her hand over Elaina's, the one that gripped her phone like a vise.

"How long was his layover? He must have just missed his connecting flight. He'll be on the next one out." Thea grabbed both of Elaina's hands. "There is a flight almost every hour from Athens to here."

Elaina loosened her grip, swiped the lock from her phone screen, and began scrolling through her contacts.

"What are you doing?" Thea asked, but she didn't answer. She found his name and pressed *call*.

It rang four times before voicemail picked up, which meant the phone was in range, an indication of being on land rather than in the air.

"It's Duncan. I'm no' answerin' because I'm on mah way to marry Elaina. So if you're no' at the wedding, then piss off for a bit while I'm with mah lady. I'll ring ya next week."

Elaina took a deep breath and a smile crossed her lips. This was a good sign, his outgoing message. He was looking forward to marrying her. Of course he was giving up a lot to be with her, but he had wanted this. He had chosen a life with her in Greece.

Then her phone buzzed with another notification. When she looked at the screen, her heart sank.

Duncan: *Forgive me. I couldn't get on the second plane.*

She waited, sure there would be more after those nine words.

One minute. Two. Three. The silence screamed as her heart sank. Then the floor dropped out from under her, and for a moment she swore she was falling. *I couldn't get on the second plane.*

Duncan was okay. He just wasn't coming to Greece, which meant…what? There was a problem with customs? He forgot something in Scotland? Or…dread weighted her stomach as she arrived at the most obvious explanation… He didn't want to marry her.

She could have made herself believe he hadn't heard the phone ring, that maybe he was waiting for better reception, or maybe he had lost his phone. But silent as it was, the text came through loud and clear.

She couldn't let Thea see her falter, couldn't let anyone see her fall apart. She had to save face and then figure out what came next. So she did what she did best and let the anger swallow the hurt.

Elaina banged her head against the door. "*Vlákas!*"

"English?" Thea said meekly, and Elaina's eyes burned.

"Stupid!" Elaina shouted. "How could I be so fucking stupid?"

She held the phone for her cousin to see.

Elaina stalked back to her dressing table. *Soft.* Thea was right. For three years she'd let Duncan, let *loving* Duncan, whittle away at her stony exterior, and how had that left her?

Vulnerable.

She thought her worries were unfounded, just pre-wedding jitters. But maybe deep below that tough exterior, her heart really had turned to marshmallow—a trusting marshmallow with a missing groom.

Well, soft was out of the fucking question now.

I am not *a marshmallow.*

She didn't even like marshmallows—Jordan made her taste some jarred version of the American treat—but that was beside the point. Elaina needed to get Duncan to Thessaloniki and soon—before she had to explain to her family *and his* why he wasn't coming. Duncan would have to tell her, face-to-face, that he was bowing out of this. *He* would have to look all their guests in the eye and explain to them why they would not be rehearsing tonight—why there would be no wedding tomorrow. Elaina may have lost the battle, but she wasn't going down with the ship.

She scrolled through her contacts once again, still ignoring Thea's confusion. As expected, *this* call went directly to voicemail. But when the plane landed, Elaina would hopefully be the first message in her queue.

"Jordan. It is Elaina. Duncan is…missing. I think he might be in Athens. I need your help to get him back here so he can leave me properly, face-to-face. Just—call me when you land. I will be here."

She collapsed into the chair, blew out a long breath, and looked at her cousin.

"Let's do this," Elaina said, grabbing Thea's makeup bag and getting to work on the dark circles under her eyes. "I want everything to be perfect today."

Thea closed her mouth, the one that had been hanging open since Elaina stood from the chair minutes ago. Then she mustered a soft, "But, Elaina—"

She cut her off.

"He needs to see what he is missing, what he is giving up, and that he did not get the best of me."

But she was sure her cousin heard the small break in her voice on that last word. Because the truth was, Duncan brought out the very best in Elaina, and she had already given those parts of herself to him. He would *always* have the best of her, but she'd never let him know.

Chapter Five

Duncan stretched as he exited the jet bridge into the terminal. He set his messenger bag down on an empty chair and turned to face the floor-to-ceiling windows and the plane from which he'd just come. As passengers disembarked, they smiled at him, and he offered the same in return.

A little more than three hours, and Scotland was gone. Just like that. His home was there, and Greece was here. The sun shone so brightly, he had to shield his eyes. That would take some getting used to. Not that Aberdeen never saw the sun, but there was something different about the sun in Greece, even in December.

Duncan wasn't visiting Greece this time. Greece was his new home. He smiled at first, but then swallowed as his throat tightened.

Greece is my new home.

For fuck's sake. Duncan lived here now. Well, not in Athens. But one more plane trip—a really freaking short one—and he'd be in Thessaloniki, which *was* his new home.

He pulled at the collar of his wool jumper, the Greek sun obviously melting him. In a swift movement, he tore off the garment, leaving only his Aberdeen Uni T-shirt and his jeans. That felt better. Of course. It was just the jumper. He could breathe now. But when he turned to the chair next to him, ready to stuff it into his messenger bag, the bag was gone.

"Bloody fucking hell," he whispered, but as he finished the phrase, he heard a squeak of rubber on tile, and he turned.

There was the thief, with Duncan's bag slung over his shoulder. The bloke from seat 23A.

"Fuck ya doin'?" Duncan yelled, and then 23A was off like a goddamn racehorse.

So was Duncan McAllister.

He was not a runner, not by choice. Duncan's idea of exercise was a slow hike up to the beach or a mental workout in front of the telly with his PlayStation. But he was suddenly a short-distance sprinter. He had his hand around the strap of the bag in less than fifteen seconds, and 23A introduced his fist to his face just as quickly.

Duncan was sure he was standing seconds ago, but now he was flat on his back, the skin and bone below his left eye throbbing and his head spinning. Over him stood a prepubescent teen and the bloke from 23A, conversing in whispered shouts.

Duncan made out, "Attacked me," and, "Detain you both for questioning," and, "Are you okay, sir?"

He thought that last one was for him, so he nodded. Not because he was okay—he was pretty fucking far from okay—but because when a stranger asked if you were okay, it was easier to say *yes* than to explain all the reasons to the contrary, and though Duncan had a growing list of why he was miles from okay, he was too dazed to voice them.

The prepubescent-looking one helped him to his feet.

The sight must have been a laugh, a git just past his A Levels lifting a twenty-five-year-old man from the ground—and quite a strapping twenty-five-year-old man, if Duncan had any say about it. Once standing, though, things went blurry. Then he swore he saw two of everything. And after that, it all went black.

D uncan sat up with a start.

"It's my bloody bag!" he called out, he realized, to an empty room. Duncan lay on a small rollaway-type bed in what looked like a doctor's examining room, his head propped on two pillows. He took a few deep breaths as his head swam. Where the hell was he?

The door opposite his bed opened, and a man dressed in all white entered carrying two miniature cups.

"For your head, Mr...." he said, smiling underneath a thick black mustache, and Duncan didn't argue. His head throbbed, so he was willing to take whatever the man was offering. He dropped two small pills in his mouth and chased them down with the water that was in the other cup.

"McAllister. Duncan McAllister."

The man nodded. "This is good," he said. "You couldn't answer that question twenty minutes ago, and you do not have ID on you, sir. We did not know who to contact."

What was this guy talking about? Of course Duncan knew his own bloody name. If only he could figure out where he was, he could be on his way to…to…

"I'm sorry, but who are *you*?" Duncan asked. *And where the hell am I meant to be?*

The man's brow furrowed, and he pulled a penlight from his pocket and clicked it on.

"If you're ready to stay awake, Mr. McAllister, I'd like to

finish your exam. We were close to sending you to hospital, but without ID it is very difficult to—"

Duncan stood, swayed, thought better of it, then dropped back on his bum on the bed.

"It's in my bag," he said, letting his head fall against the pillows again. He was so close to surrendering, to letting his eyes close, when he bolted upright again.

"Christ, what did that arsehole do to me?" It all came flooding back—the plane, his seatmate running off with his bag, his head hitting the floor.

What time was it? Had he missed his connecting flight? Did Elaina know where he was?

"I have a concussion, aye?" he asked. This was no doctor's office. He knew that now. It was some makeshift clinic or first-aid station. God, if they'd sent him to hospital, he'd be filling out paperwork the rest of the day. "Wouldn't be my first," he joked. "If you could get my bag, I'll give you ID, whatever you need. I just have to catch my next plane. Getting married tomorrow."

The doctor, nurse, clinician—whoever he was—forced a smile. Duncan squinted to read the name on his tag—*Feodor*.

"I am sorry, Mr. McAllister. But your bag—the bag that was found on the other gentleman—is being detained. And so are you."

Duncan sat up. "I'm sorry, what? Detained? Brilliant. That bastard takes my bag, knocks me the fuck out, and you're detaining *me*?" He rubbed the back of his neck and blinked hard, trying to clear his vision only to realize it was the swelling in his left eye that was making things all wonky. "Show me where my bag is being held bloody prisoner, and I'll prove to you lot that it's mine, and then I'll be on my way. To get *married*."

The resolve in Duncan's voice impressed even him. It's not like he was having second thoughts, but give a bloke a minute or two to collect himself when he's up and leaving one home for another. That's all he had done when he got off that plane, and look where it had gotten him. But he was sure now, no doubt in his mind, that this was where he belonged. Greece was where he belonged. Because Greece was where Elaina was, and *she* was his new home.

He scrambled for his phone in his front pocket. At least that wasn't detained with everything else. When he unlocked the screen, he cursed at himself when he saw his nearly dead battery. Elaina insisted he wait until Greece to get a new phone on a local carrier, which was all fine and good except that his old phone barely held a charge anymore. Of course he had his charger with him—in his bag. Duncan wasn't sure what Elaina was thinking at this point, but he had to let her know he was all right, that he was on his way. He saw he'd missed a call from her, but there wasn't enough battery to check his voicemail and get a message to her, so he opted for the text.

Forgive me. I couldn't get on the second plane.

The battery flashed red. *Fuck.* He wasn't done typing, but he had to hit send and hope this was enough until he got to her.

It was more than an hour after he was supposed to get on that second plane when Duncan could finally walk without fear of blacking out again.

"It's *my* bag," he insisted as soon as he was seated across the table from the man who'd stolen it.

The security bloke, the one he vaguely remembered from before he was knocked bloody unconscious, slid his bag toward him on the table. Duncan squinted with his good eye at the guy's name tag—*Kostas.*

"Then I'm sure you can unlock it," he said to Duncan. "This one says he shouldn't have to without us providing him with legal aide, but if you feel differently—"

Duncan snatched the bag. Of course he felt differently. He'd open it, show everyone his passport, and end this bleeding cock-up of a morning.

He rolled the numbers into place, giving himself a mental pat on the back for programming the lock's combination to tomorrow's date, his wedding date.

The thirty-first of December. New Year's Eve, the last time they'd be Duncan McAllister and Elaina Tripoli. The day she'd take his name.

3-1-1-2. And *click.*

Where was the click?

He reset the lock and rolled the barrels into place again. 3-1-1-2.

Nothing.

He tried reversing the order. Maybe he'd done it the American way with the month first.

1-2-3-1.

Duncan gave the lock a violent yank. He shook the bag. *My fucking bag.*

"Cut it off," he said through gritted teeth. "It's broken. Cut the thing off, and I'll show you it's mine. I can tell you everything in there, including my bloody passport. Just cut. It. Off."

Kostas retrieved the bag.

"That's the next step, sir, since it looks like *your* bag doesn't want to open for you. But I have to find a tool that will cut a small padlock."

Duncan ran a hand through his hair, wanting to yank it out. "A bolt cutter. You need a bleedin' bolt cutter."

Kostas nodded, and Duncan was sure the kid had no clue

what a bolt cutter was or where to get one. This was a joke, right? A pre-wedding laugh at his expense. Yet no one was smiling.

"I should get a phone call, aye? One call?" This would be his last chance to get word out to someone who could end this ridiculous morning.

Kostas raised his brows and said, "Yes! Like an American crime show!"

"My phone is dead," Duncan told him. "I'm going to need yours."

Kostas seemed all too eager to hand Duncan his phone, enjoying what must be the most excitement he'd had since starting his job.

Duncan rolled his eyes, but to be honest, that's where the idea of the phone call came from. All that mattered was that Kostas said *yes*. As much as he wanted to phone Elaina and explain everything to her, she had the whole wedding party to attend to. He couldn't ask her to help him. But he could call Griffin. Griffin would be getting to Thessaloniki soon, if he wasn't already there.

Shite. What was his number? Duncan's phone was crap with international calls, so he always had to type the number in when he used his international phone card. He squeezed his eyes shut, head and cheek still throbbing, and concentrated. He wasn't even sure he'd get through, but he had to try.

"Yes!" he yelled as the numbers came to him, and he tapped the keypad furiously as Kostas and the bloke from 23A stared on.

The call went right to voicemail, but Griffin would have to be in range soon, right?

"Oi, mate," Duncan began. "I'm in a right mess at the moment and was hoping you could help. Athens airport, security holding cell number one. I owe ya one. I'll explain when you get here. If you get here. Shite, can you get here?"

Duncan ended the call but snuck in a quick text to Noah as well, his brain suddenly swimming with numbers, Elaina's included. He could go for broke if Kostas didn't notice, try to explain the situation, to assure her he was only delayed but that he was trying to get to her.

But how did he put it all in a text from someone else's phone? What would he say? That he let his nerves get the best of him, enough so that he didn't see his bag being stolen by the wanker still claiming it was his?

He had spent years proving to Elaina that he wasn't the boy who stole a birthday kiss that night in the pub. He was the man she'd always known he could be. But if she saw him right now, she'd run in the opposite direction, and he couldn't blame her. Only a boy could fuck up as much as he had in such a short amount of time, and if he didn't get that bag back, there would be no point in showing up in Thessaloniki today. There'd be no point in any of it.

But before he could even type out her number, Kostas snatched the phone back from him.

"One call," the lanky git said. "How about you?" Kostas asked the real thief, but the guy just grunted out a *no*.

This was it. Duncan was so close to where he needed to be yet so very far away. All he knew was that *nothing* about today felt like home.

Chapter Six

Maggie

Maggie adjusted the small airplane pillow against the window and stretched as best she could in the confined space. It took her a few blinks to open her eyes completely, and when she did, Griffin's soft gaze was on her, those caramel eyes drinking her in.

"What?" she asked, sure that he'd caught her snoring or drooling, which really wouldn't be that big of a deal. He'd seen her at her worst and still taken on the challenge of loving her. Maggie had to remind herself that she didn't have to be anyone but herself with him. She could just *be*.

He lifted the armrests that formed the barrier between them, then took her left leg and draped it over his right. Griffin let out a sigh and smiled.

"Don't move," she said, and then pulled her camera from the seatback pocket. Something about the way he looked at her made her want to capture this moment.

He chuckled as she snapped the photo.

"I'm glad you got some rest, but I have a confession," he said, a glint in his eyes that made something in her gut tighten.

"What's that?"

He traced circles on her thigh, sparks bypassing the thin blanket and then the denim covering her skin, traveling straight through her core. She squirmed, and his grin broadened, eyes crinkling with delight.

"I may have been fantasizing a bit about what we could do when you woke up."

His hand was under the blanket now, her jeans the only thing standing between his skin and hers.

"On…on the plane?" she asked, willing him both to stop and to keep driving her insane. "But I've been sleeping for, like, three hours. I'm all travel gross and have morning mouth. Or afternoon mouth. What time zone are we in?" She gasped on that last word as Griffin's fingers dipped under the hem of her sweater, the tips brushing the bare skin of her belly.

She stood abruptly, her head bumping the air blower thingy. Griffin laughed.

"I need to freshen up. Or something. I need to… I'm gonna… Can you grab my carry-on from the overhead bin?"

Griffin stood next to her, resting one knee on his seat to accommodate for his height and save him from head-butting the ceiling as she had. He kissed her softly on the jaw, just below her ear. His late-night or early-morning stubble—Jesus, what time was it?—tickled her skin, and there were those sparks again. God, what she wouldn't do for this man, but not before assessing the situation. And besides, what were they going to do on a plane? People didn't really…

"I'll meet you in there in five," he whispered, interrupting her internal monologue. His breath warmed her skin, his voice low and gruff and, *shit*, so sexy.

"K," was all she could manage because, omigod, people really did that? On planes? That was his fantasy…and apparently hers now, too.

Griffin stepped out into the aisle, opening the bin to retrieve her bag.

"Oooh, perfect timing!" Jordan said, popping up from her seat to stand next to him. "Can you grab mine, too? I'm hungry."

"I've got it!" Noah sprang up as well, nailing his head as Maggie had.

They all shared a collective laugh, and Maggie's heart raced as she grabbed her bag and headed to the back of the plane. Once in the tiny bathroom—door left unlocked—she studied herself in the mirror.

So much had changed in a year, and Griffin was the catalyst for that change—for getting her to step outside the safe zone. After hiding herself away, hiding how she'd had to alter her lifestyle to compensate for the new way her brain worked, she had finally let Griffin in fully and completely. She had loved and trusted and let herself be loved in return, and it had gotten her to where they now were.

She blinked at her reflection. The skin under her eyes was a little darker than normal, but Maggie Kendall was smiling because she was on a plane to another country, so far from safe she couldn't even see it anymore, and it felt *good*.

The door opened, and she gasped when she saw an older man recoil at the bathroom not being vacant.

"Sorry!" she yelped, heart pounding, and then she giggled. "Occupied."

The man grunted a sound of disapproval. "Lock the door, then," he grumbled. "Why doesn't anyone lock the door?"

She pulled the unlocked door shut again and waited for Griffin. She hadn't realized it until she met him, but she had spent two years waiting. Waiting for life to return to normal. Waiting to be the girl she was at nineteen, the one who hadn't suffered a traumatic brain injury and undergone surgery that left her scarred in ways no one could see but her. Griffin never knew that Maggie, and a part of her wished he could have. Another part still waited for normal, a word that would never exist in their shared vocabulary.

"Stop psyching yourself out, Mags," she said to the girl in the mirror. "He loves and trusts the *you* you are now."

The problem, though, was that Maggie was still learning to do the same. This weekend would be the test. If she could survive the flight, the jet lag, the extra stimulation of places and people she didn't know, then maybe she could trust in a future that was less than safe.

Right now she just had to trust that the next person to open that door would be Griffin, and with that trust she let the worry fall away, replaced with thoughts of his lips on hers and his hands on her skin.

The girl in the mirror smiled back.

"Nope," she said aloud, biting her lip. "What we're about to do in this closet of a room falls nowhere under my definition of safe. Not at all."

Chapter Seven

NOAH

He watched Griffin eye Maggie as she headed to the back of the plane before he sat down again in their row. Then Noah followed suit, collapsing into the seat next to Jordan with a sigh.

"Hey," she started. "What's wrong?" She ripped open a package of almonds and offered him one, but he shook his head.

How could he explain how being here with her and Griffin brought him back three years—to watching her with him while Noah made mistake after mistake, pushing her away. It wasn't that he was still jealous of Griffin dating Jordan first. Okay, fine. He was a little jealous. Seeing the guy who got to be with her when Noah couldn't? He blamed himself for losing that first chance with her, but being around Griffin—he felt that loss all over again. He still felt it was pure luck that she hadn't written him off by the time he found her in London just before New Year's Eve, that she fought hard enough to break through his trust barriers so they could get to where they were now. Even though it had been three years, Noah still worried that he'd somehow mess up again, that he'd lose his best friend—the person who filled the spaces in his heart he never knew were there until he met Brooks on that train. How the hell did he put all that into words that would explain that when it came to their past, he'd always want to prove to her that she made the right choice.

Noah pushed the armrest up and hooked a finger into Jordan's belt loop, urging her closer.

"You know," he said, his lips brushing her ear as he spoke in a soft whisper. "I could meet you back there. If you want."

Jordan sucked in a sharp breath, and he smiled. Maybe he couldn't put into words what kept eating away at him, but he could do everything in his power to make this trip perfect, to make sure Jordan knew how important she was to him.

At first she only nodded, and he grinned against her, sliding his hand from her belt loop to her thigh, the tips of his fingers disappearing between her legs.

"Noah." His name was a whispered plea, and he realized this was how to say what he couldn't articulate. He pressed a finger against her center, massaged her through her jeans, and Jordan squirmed in her seat. *"Noah,"* she said again, and this time it was a reprimand, yet one that was accompanied by her gorgeous smile.

"Head on back there," he said softly, his voice doing nothing to hide his need for the woman sitting next to him. "I'm right behind you."

She stuffed the almonds back into her bag and shoved it under the seat. Then she kissed him before stepping into the aisle and disappearing toward the back of the plane. He stayed facing forward, not wanting to be obvious, and counted to sixty. Twice. And then he couldn't wait any longer.

Noah took a deep breath and relaxed as his eyes took in the green vacant sign. She'd left the door unlocked for him. They were going to do this. And he *could* do this. Confined spaces had become less of a threat when Jordan was around. Just being in her presence calmed him, as if her frenetic energy drew out the opposite from him. Plus, how bad could a small space be when her delicious skin was on his?

He threw open the door and stepped inside, only to find the vacant sign was telling the truth. Jordan wasn't there. He moved to back out of the space, realizing he'd chosen the wrong door, just as another passenger backed into him and slammed the door shut. Noah pitched forward over the small excuse for a counter, his forehead slamming into the mirror. This didn't surprise him. Physical injury brought on by his often clumsy girlfriend was fairly common—and to Noah, endearing—though Jordan didn't usually hit with this much force.

"Oh shit."

Though the stars hadn't yet cleared his vision, Noah knew that voice, and it sure as hell wasn't Jordan's. When he straightened himself to full standing position and focused on the mirror, he took in the sight of Griffin standing behind him, *right* behind him, with barely room to breathe, his head thrown back in laughter against the door. The closed door.

"What are you doing?" Noah asked.

"Same thing as you, I'd guess," Griffin said, taking no notice of Noah's palms gripping the counter, knuckles white against the dulled silver. "Guess I should have paid better attention. I totally thought Maggie went right, but she must have gone left." He laughed harder. "And Jordan's gotta be in the one just next to us. Jesus, we're a couple of assholes. I'm sorry, man."

Griffin spun back to face the door, nudging at the lock. Once. Then twice. Then Noah watched as his fellow occupant's fist curved around the small bolt, struggling to pull it free.

Noah ran his hand through his hair as his throat tightened.

"You've got to fucking be kidding me," he said. "This is *not* happening."

Noah turned toward the door and pushed Griffin to the side against the toilet so he could wedge himself in front of the door, slamming the heel of his palm against the stubborn bolt. Nothing.

He backed away, sliding into a sitting position on the counter, the only way to give himself a few inches to breathe.

"What the hell did you do?" he asked, observing as Griffin's eyes widened. Noah pressed one hand to his chest and the other out in front of him, trying to force an arm's length between them.

"You're having a panic attack," Griffin said, the realization evident in the words.

Noah closed his eyes and took in a long, slow breath, a calming mechanism he hadn't needed in quite some time. He nodded but focused on his breathing before saying anything else.

"Look, Reed, I appreciate you stating the obvious, but let's just get the fuck out of here. Okay?" he said through labored breaths.

Griffin's shoulders slumped as he pressed himself back against the door. Noah could tell he was trying to create more space, and he had to give the guy credit for that.

"Hold on a sec," Noah said, remembering the back door to his and Jordan's apartment, the one they rarely used because the door was misaligned and the lock always got stuck.

He hopped off the counter, and Griffin wedged himself into the corner, not that it mattered. Their shoulders still touched, but Noah didn't have time to care. He grabbed the small door handle and pulled the door toward the inner frame and then tried the lock again. Nothing. So he pushed the door into the outer frame and tugged at the bolt again.

Freedom.

He popped the door open and stumbled into the slightly larger space between the four bathrooms. *Four* bathrooms? Well, that explained his misjudgment. He'd pay better attention next time. Fuck, who was he kidding? There would be no next time. He was pretty sure sweaty palms and uneven breathing *before* the good stuff even started would not be the way to get Jordan to scream his name—in pleasure, that is. She'd probably scream her head off if he blacked out before she even got his pants unzipped.

"How'd you know?" he asked Griffin before they headed back to their seats. "That it was a panic attack."

Griffin shrugged. "Maggie has similar symptoms sometimes, before a migraine comes on. I'd do anything to keep that from ever happening to her again, but I can't take it away from her, you know? It sucks, and I'm sorry it happens to you, too."

Noah had to hand it to him. Griffin was a good guy. That's part of the reason Noah had such a hard time being around him. When he'd met Jordan on the train to Scotland three years ago, he fell for her almost instantly. But because his ex was with him on the exchange program, things got complicated quickly, and Jordan ended up dating Griffin for their first few months in Aberdeen. He was good to Jordan. And even though things didn't work out because, despite their rocky beginning, Jordan had fallen for Noah as quickly as he'd fallen for her, she and Griffin parted as friends and were still pretty close.

If Griffin had been an ass, it would have been easier for him to just let it go. But *Noah* was the ass, the one who almost missed out on being with the person he loved most; he'd be a dick to hold his own mistakes against Griffin. It was time to let it go.

"Thanks? I guess," Noah said. "Are we having a moment or something?"

Griffin laughed. "I think we are." He paused for a second. "You were going to risk that for Jordan?"

Noah laughed, too. "Yeah. I was. But I'm officially reconsidering."

Griffin held out his hand, and Noah gripped it in a firm shake.

"Leave the past in the past?" Griffin asked.

Noah let out a long breath, and with it he released three-year-old doubt and regret.

"Leave the past in the past."

Chapter Eight

Miles

If sitting seventeen rows behind Griffin, Maggie, Jordan, and Noah *plus* getting stuck in the middle of a three-seat row didn't make Miles a fifth wheel, he didn't know what did. He knew he shouldn't be sulking. He did get a great deal on the ticket, after all. But he also knew from watching Maggie and Jordan glide past him to the cluster of lavatories in the back of the plane, and Griffin and Noah scrutinizing their every move, that there was a whole lotta somethin' going on, and he would be the only one this weekend getting nothing.

The woman to his left had slept most of the flight but now was leaning across the aisle, conversing with the man in the opposite row's window seat. Greek was a loud language. Or maybe she just had to shout to make her voice reach beyond not only the expanse of the aisle but also the poor guy sitting on the end seat. Miles couldn't get a good look at him past the woman's animated gesticulations, but he could tell the passenger was smiling, and he liked that this stranger was just as amused by the conversation as he was.

Sleep never came easily for Miles, and he had whiled away the hours either feigning the activity or reading the romance novel he ended up running back to Hudson News to purchase. What could he say? He judged books by their covers, and this one had him at a half-naked couple. Turned out the story was pretty good, too, if you were into happily-ever-afters and all that crap.

A third voice joined the cross-aisle convo, and moments later the woman next to Miles was standing up, repeating a word he didn't understand.

"*Efharistó*," she said to the man across the aisle as he rose along with her. "*Efharistó*."

And then she was in his seat, and he was in hers, and Miles was—staring. Except Miles Parker didn't stare. He was the object of *other* people's gawks and ogles, men and women alike. It's not like he was an asshole about his looks, but he never put on the bullshit of false modesty. He was hot. He knew it. And he liked the effect it had on others.

"It means *thank you*."

Miles was sure the guy had some sort of European accent, but it was too slight to place. What he was more concerned about was the fullness of the lips from which the accented voice came.

"How did you know I spoke English?" Miles asked, finding his voice.

Those lips turned up into a sinful grin, and Miles followed the corners of the man's mouth to the apples of his cheeks and the crinkle of his cinnamon-colored eyes.

Again with the *staring*.

"I was watching you speak to those American girls who walked by just before. The one with the red hair—she is your girlfriend?"

Miles grinned at the thought of being watched. Then he

chuckled at the question. He *was*, technically, Maggie's plus-one for the wedding. He loved her more than anyone else he knew. And yet, the answer was an emphatic *no*.

The stranger's thick, dark brows furrowed, and for a second Miles let his gaze drift to the passengers coming up the aisle. He nodded as Griffin and Noah passed them by, confirming his suspicions.

Still laughing, Miles said, "The lighter-haired one, *that* is the boyfriend."

His new seatmate narrowed his eyes. "Then can I admit something?" he asked, and Miles crossed his arms over his chest.

"Sure. I like admissions."

Mystery Man scrubbed a hand across the dark stubble on his jaw.

"I noticed you at the gate at JFK."

Miles sighed. "My apologies, then."

"For what?"

"For being too wrapped up in the first pity party I'd thrown myself in a long time to notice you. Because I do now, and let me tell you…you're hard not to notice."

He held out his hand toward Miles and started, "I'm—"

But Miles shook his head. "No names," he said. "What would be the point?"

The guy shrugged and laughed. "I guess there isn't one." He turned then to face the passenger in front of him, reclining his seat and resting his hands behind his head as if he were lounging at the beach.

Miles followed suit.

Shit.

There was a beautiful, way-too-charming man sitting next to him, and Miles just gave him the polite *fuck off*. When did he ever shy away from flirting? This was the fun part. But something about this guy set off an internal alarm, one Miles couldn't recognize or define.

"You know," Mystery Man said, still staring at the cabin's ceiling, "we don't need to share names to make a good time of the rest of the flight."

Miles agreed to himself that this was a good point. He should explore it further.

"What did you have in mind?" he asked.

"Another admission," the man said. "When I saw you at JFK, I wondered what it would be like to kiss you." He leaned closer, enough so that Miles could feel his breath on his own lips. "Do you wonder what it would be like to kiss me?"

Well, he sure as hell was wondering that now.

"I bet you say that to all the men you meet on airplanes," Miles teased, aiming for the casual confidence he usually oozed, but his heart rate increased. He decided to write it off as arousal. After all, he hadn't been with anyone since Paige, and the man next to him was quite the specimen. Maggie wanted him to let go this weekend and enjoy himself, and here he was being offered the chance for some guaranteed enjoyment.

"I do," Miles said, imagining what the lips so close to his would taste like. "But I've never been one for putting on a show."

Without another word, the man whose name he desperately didn't want to know stood from his seat and headed toward the final rows of the plane—and the cluster of lavatories that lay beyond.

Miles felt his dick strain against his jeans, the sensation silencing any sort of warning he'd tried to give himself moments before.

He shook his head and grinned, then followed his seatmate to the tail of the aircraft.

After all, a fifth wheel never said no to a sixth, especially when they both seemed to want—or in Miles's case *need*—

the same thing. A release, something to push the past back to its hiding place in favor of pure physical desire. It's not like he was a stranger to random hookups, and this one had the promise of no repercussions. When the plane landed, Miles would be on his way, and so would the man with no name. For now, he could stand a little pleasure before a weekend that only promised the reminder of emotional pain.

He barely got the door shut and bolted behind him before Mystery Man's lips crashed against his. He'd been anticipating how those lips would taste from the second the guy sat down next to him, and the reality did *not* fall short of the fantasy.

Coffee and something sweet, like he'd just stepped out of a patisserie or some other European-sounding bakery, not like he'd been languishing for hours on a plane, breathing the same recirculated air as hundreds of others.

If this was his first taste of Europe, Miles wasn't complaining.

He nipped at that full bottom lip, then took in a sharp breath as a strong hand palmed him where he throbbed inside his jeans.

Fuck the playful nipping. Miles felt those lips part against his, and he kissed his delicious stranger hard and deep as the hand on top of his zipper slid down, fingers cupping him firmly as Miles tried to keep his knees from buckling.

He let out a low growl and ran his hands through the thick caramel hair he wanted so desperately to touch.

Miles wasn't a stranger to casual sex, but there was something agonizing about not knowing this guy's name, even if it had been his own idea to keep names out of this. A name alone was the shallowest form of identity, yet it established a connection. Whatever happened on this plane, when they disembarked, it would be over. No name. No way to find each other again.

Miles spun his man of mystery so his torso lay pressed

against the door. Taut biceps flexed under the tanned skin of his arms. He splayed his palm between his shoulder blades, the man's thin T-shirt leaving very little to the imagination.

He rocked his pelvis into the small of the stranger's back and groaned as those tawny arms lifted so his hands could spread against the pocket door. He was letting Miles take the lead.

Miles reached around to find his companion rock hard inside his well-worn jeans, and without warning, the words just fell out.

"I need to know your—"

The lavatory door flew open, and both Miles and the other man tumbled into the cabin, nearly bulldozing Miles's former seatmate. Passengers in the rearmost seats turned toward the commotion, and Miles did exactly what typical Miles would do in this situation. He smiled, and then he bowed.

"...name," Miles said under his breath. "I need to know your name."

"*Sygnómi! Sygnómi!*"

His fellow occupant chuckled and took it all in stride as the Greek woman kept repeating, over and over until she was locked safely in the lavatory, "*Sygnómi! Sygnómi!*"

"She's saying she's sorry," the man with no identity said, and Miles shook his head and let out a relieved laugh.

Thank you, he thought as he glanced back at the lavatory door. *You saved me from myself.*

He was about to turn back toward the cabin when he noticed a rectangle of paper on the floor. His almost-mile-high partner was already heading back toward their seats. Because he hadn't thought that paper was there before, he bent down and picked it up. Only when he read it did he realize he should have left the trash pickup to those in charge.

Because Miles couldn't unread what he read, couldn't unknow what he knew. So he stared at the business card again.

Alexander Karas. Sous Chef. Ambrosia Café.
Thessaloniki

"Are you coming?"

The question sounded like it wasn't the first time being asked, and Miles realized Alexander must have come back to check on him.

Alexander. Alex. He was totally an Alex. Miles could feel it.

He shoved the card in his front pocket and turned to face the man he was sure he was connected to by so much more than a name now.

"Yeah. Sorry. I'm, uh, gonna head up front for a bit and see my friends. See you in a few?"

Alex smiled. "I'll save your seat."

And without another word, he sat back down as Miles did his best not to look like he was rushing to Maggie—but he needed two questions answered, and she would know the first one.

He found her lounging against the window next to her seat, a sleeping Griffin resting his head on her shoulder.

"You look...rumpled," Maggie said. "You never look rumpled." She narrowed her eyes. "What were you doing, Miles Parker?"

He shook his head a little too violently, but *fuck*, she didn't know how important this was.

"Mags...what's the name of Elaina's family's restaurant?"

She pursed her lips and squinted her eyes.

"You know how much I suck at restaurant names, sweetie. They kind of get filed as unnecessary in the short-term memory department. I can ask Griffin when he wakes up."

"Hey, what am I? Invisible?"

Miles turned to where he swore Jordan was sleeping just seconds ago.

"Ambrosia," she said. "Ambrosia Café."

Question number two—would Miles and Alex be able to leave the plane as strangers, safe from seeing each other again? The odds weren't looking good.

Maybe it was a good thing the lavatory door wasn't properly locked and things ended before they went too far.

He knew what Maggie would say if he explained. She'd call it serendipity, say it was meant to be just like when she met Griffin. But serendipity didn't apply to him, even if knowing Alex's name only made him want to know more. What would be the point in getting to know a man who lived thousands of miles away? What good would it do to even consider what someone like Alex would think about someone like him?

He didn't know the answers to those questions, only that they were pushing through all the barriers he'd spent so long constructing.

One thing was for sure. Miles was screwed.

Chapter Nine

GRIFFIN

When the seat-belt sign finally turned off, everyone stood and stretched. Griffin popped open the overhead bin, but he waited for Noah to take down his and Jordan's bags before retrieving Maggie's and his own. Noah gave him a tired half smile, acknowledgment that the truce was still in place, and Griffin let out a long breath.

It was still hard for Griffin to see the change in himself since Aberdeen. Waking up next to Maggie every day was a good reminder. So was going to a job that paid him barely enough to live on yet fulfilled him more than he could have imagined. Being offered the fellowship—he still couldn't wrap his brain around that. And he still hadn't told Maggie.

"You okay, Fancy Pants?"

Griffin snapped out of his daze to find both hands gripping the frame of the carry-on bin, yet he hadn't made a move to actually bring their bags down to their seats. He grabbed Maggie's first and handed it to her.

"Sorry. Just jet-lagged, I guess." He slung his bag over his shoulder and across his torso. Then he pulled Maggie close, burying his face in her hair as he kissed the top of her head. "And I should be the one checking in on *you*."

The passengers in front of them began to move, so Maggie didn't have a chance to respond. Instead, she threaded her fingers through Griffin's as they exited the plane, single file. Once out in the open air of the gate, the four of them stopped and waited for Miles. He walked off the jet bridge a few minutes later. But as Miles veered from the stream of passengers who were heading straight to baggage claim, the guy behind him followed him over to the group.

"Hey, guys," Miles said, and Griffin cleared his throat, nodding just past Miles's shoulder.

They all watched him turn toward the man who put his hand on Miles's neck, pulled his head close, and whispered something in his ear.

"I know," Miles said, loud enough for all of them to hear.

"Miles, sweetie," Maggie said. "You gonna introduce us to your friend?"

Griffin watched the muscle in Miles's jaw clench. He was no stranger to that almost inconspicuous tic; it was especially prevalent when Griffin first met Maggie and Miles regarded him as a threat to her happiness—and rightfully so. They were friends now, and Griffin knew the tension Miles was trying to hide was not meant for Maggie.

"Miles," the stranger said, a grin spreading across his face. "Well, it was nice to meet you, Miles." And then he kissed him, nodded to the group, and left the five of them standing there, jaws on the floor.

Miles grabbed his rolling carry-on. "Shall we?" he asked, and strode past them all.

They stood at the baggage carousel waiting for the final bag of the group—Jordan's suitcase.

"It's because it probably exploded," she joked.

"Oh shit," Griffin said as Jordan's bag finally made its way around. As soon as he'd taken his phone off airplane mode, a voicemail had popped up. He listened to it now.

"What?" she asked him.

"What's up?" Noah echoed.

"Have either of you turned on your phones yet?"

Jordan and Noah both retrieved their phones, her from her purse and Noah from his pocket.

"Oh shit," Noah said when he looked at his screen.

"*Shit* is right," Jordan replied as she listened to her voicemail that Griffin was sure was from Elaina.

"What's going on?" Maggie asked.

Miles joined in. "Am I missing something?"

"Duncan's missing," Jordan said. "Elaina thinks he's standing her up."

Noah shook his head. "I don't think he is."

"Me, either," said Griffin.

Noah handed Jordan his phone so she could read the text.

I'm in the Athens airport. Need your help.

Then Griffin handed her his, letting her listen to his voicemail.

"Oi, mate. I'm in a right mess at the moment and was hoping you could help. Athens airport, security holding cell number one. I owe ya one. I'll explain when you get here. If you get here. Shite, can you get here?"

Jordan gave the phone back to Griffin, and he glanced at Noah, who nodded in silent agreement.

"Can someone please tell me what the hell is going on here?" Miles asked. "I'd kind of like in on the drama."

Maggie grabbed his hand. "You gonna tell us about that

kiss? Because—*hello*? Drama?"

Miles rolled his eyes, and Jordan spoke up.

"Duncan is missing, but he's not standing Elaina up. He's in some kind of trouble in the Athens airport."

Griffin kissed Maggie on the cheek and then bit his lip before speaking.

"And Noah and I need to go get him."

His heart sank as he watched Maggie's eyes widen.

"You're leaving?" she asked, and Griffin understood the fear in her voice. Maggie was in a strange place with people she barely knew.

Jordan grabbed Maggie's free hand. "I'll take good care of her, Griff. You guys just take care of each other."

"You're cool if we go?" Noah asked, and Jordan nodded.

"Of course. I just don't get why he didn't call Elaina. Her first couple of messages were really frantic, but then the last two were eerily calm, saying stuff about accepting his choice but wanting him to see what he's missing."

Noah ran a hand through his hair and laughed.

"What's so funny?" Jordan asked.

"Brooks, do you remember when you introduced me to Elaina?" She nodded. "Look, I love her and everything, but she threatened to kill me in my sleep if I hurt you."

Griffin chuckled. "Why do you think I drank her Turkish coffee? I was more afraid of the consequences of *not* drinking it than what it would taste like."

"She's scary, Brooks. And I think Duncan's scared that he fucked this all up."

Noah pulled her from the group and wrapped her in a hug.

Griffin cupped Maggie's face in his palms, and she held tight to his wrists, cutting him off before he could speak.

"I'm okay, Fancy Pants."

He sighed, leaning down to press his forehead against

hers.

"This wasn't the plan, you know," he said. "To drag you thousands of miles from home and then abandon you."

Maggie chuckled. "You'll be gone a few hours, right? I promise I won't break that quickly."

He loved her for reassuring him, but it was also because he loved her that he could hear the slight waver in her voice, the tiny bit of worry she couldn't hide, and it made saying good-bye to her all that much harder.

"You've got your meds?" he asked, and Maggie stepped back, rolling her eyes.

"I'm a big girl, Griffin. I can take care of myself. Been doing it for years." She nodded toward Miles. "Plus, you're not leaving me alone. I've got him."

Griffin groaned. He didn't mean to sound like a parent leaving a child home alone for the first time. Of course she could take care of herself, but he was on new ground here, not sure how to proceed. Things were supposed to go off without a hitch—a great trip that would buoy his confidence enough to tell Maggie that he applied for a fellowship, won said fellowship, and was expected to move to Washington, D.C., this fall. No big deal.

Shit. Every time he thought about telling her, something got in the way. Or maybe he let things get in the way because, right now, avoiding the inevitable was preferable to the inevitable itself.

He was an idiot.

"I'm sorry," he said. "I'm an asshole. I know you'll be fine. I just—I wasn't expecting to have to leave you, you know?"

He grabbed her hand and pulled her to him, wrapping his arms around her waist.

"I know," Maggie said with a sigh. "It's okay. I love you for worrying about me. I just wish you didn't have to."

She wrapped her arms around his neck and stood on her

toes to kiss him, and he sank into her, his shoulders relaxing as he tried to drink his fill. He might be an idiot, but he wasn't stupid. He'd never have enough of Maggie, would never grow tired of the wholeness he felt only when he was with her.

D.C. wouldn't happen without her. It couldn't.

"I love you," he whispered.

"Love you, too," she said.

He heard a throat clear and turned to see Jordan and Noah.

"Uh, sorry," Noah said. "But if we want to catch the next flight to Athens, we need to go now."

"I like this," Jordan said, looking at the two men. "You guys are like partners or something. No, you're like Athos and Porthos going to save Aramis!"

"Excuse me?" Griffin said.

Noah chuckled. "The Three Musketeers."

"You two seem different," Maggie said, pointing back and forth between Griffin and Noah.

"Yeah," Jordan agreed, crossing her arms. "What happened with you two when Maggie and I—uh—went to the bathroom?"

Griffin maintained his poker face and shrugged. "Already told ya. We got stuck behind the drink cart."

Noah nodded slowly. "What he said."

"Well," Jordan continued, "whatever's going on with you two, it's really sweet what you're doing, saving the groom and all."

"Guess we're off to book a flight," Griffin said. "Athens is only an hour away. We can get there for a hundred bucks each and hopefully get Duncan on the next flight out."

"Elaina is only about twenty minutes from here. The three of us will hop in a taxi and help her salvage the rest of the day," Jordan told them.

"And we'll be back in time for the rehearsal dinner,"

Noah said.

"Did you say Elaina lived by her family's restaurant?" Miles asked, and Jordan nodded.

"Apartment right above it, why?"

"Just curious," he added.

"I feel like we need to do an official huddle or something," Maggie said.

And just like that, they all thrust a hand into the center of the circle in which they already stood.

"Operation Save the Groom is on, starting...now!" Griffin said, and each one of them threw their hand in the air.

"You know what they say about the best-laid plans?" Miles asked before the group dispersed.

"What's that?" Jordan asked.

He shook his head. "Fuck the planning, because it always comes back to bite you in the ass."

Maggie giggled. "And you thought you weren't part of the drama, Miles."

Griffin expelled a sigh of relief. Maggie would be fine. They'd all be fine.

He watched as Miles and Maggie helped Jordan grab Griffin's and Noah's checked bags to take with them to Elaina's, and he and Noah were off, headed toward the ticketing counter while the others made their way outside.

No more excuses. Griffin didn't want anything coming back to bite him in the ass, so he made himself a promise to come clean with Maggie tonight.

Chapter Ten

Airport Security Officer Kostas left the room to fetch a coffee for each of his alleged transgressors. He may have been shite in the crime-solving department, but at least he had the decency to offer Duncan and the arsehole refreshments.

Duncan splayed his hands on the table in front of him and stared hard at the real culprit across from him.

"It's mine, ya right bawbag. You ken it is. Just give it to me, and let me get to my wedding."

The guy he'd spent the flight from Scotland to Athens with finally spoke.

"I was just protecting myself, aye. You'd have done the same if someone chased you through an airport."

Duncan growled. The bloke was Scottish as well, and Duncan hated him even more because of it. He could have been kin. Shite, what if he was? His mum could have invited a cousin or two he didn't know.

He shook the thought away. "*I* was protecting what

belongs to *me.*"

Duncan's cheek throbbed. His head ached. For fuck's sake, he was not the kind of bloke who got into a fight unless he was too piss-drunk to realize it, and that only happened once. Okay, twice if you count the time he and his cousin Ewan were so drunk they decided to box for sport and Duncan cracked a knuckle on Ewan's jaw. But shite, who gets clotheslined in an airport on the way to his own wedding?

Duncan did, and Elaina would never forgive him for it. His only hope of righting the situation was getting his damned bag back. Then she'd understand.

"Maybe it is yours," the arse said. "But maybe I thought it was mine, and got scared, and—" The guy paused. "Where's my legal aide? I shouldn't be talking any more without an aide."

"Just shut it," Duncan said through gritted teeth, and the man leaned back in his chair, looking patient as could be. Now that he had shut up, though, the silence roared in the tiny room, or maybe that was just Duncan's pulse.

Kostas walked back in with two small Styrofoam cups and handed one to each of the men at the table.

"Wha' about the bolt cutter? Better yet, can I take my bag and go now?" Duncan asked, just to annoy the kid whose answer was already clear.

"I'm sorry, Mr. McAllister," he said in accented English. "I saw you assail this man and he defend himself. While your version of the story makes sense as well, I know what I saw. So until we can open the bag, I have to detain you both. I'm just waiting on my manager to find something we can use to cut the lock. Or we could just cut open the bag."

"No!" Duncan yelled. "Christ. I asked you to cut off the bloody lock, not ruin the bag and most likely what's inside it." He rolled his eyes. This wanker thought he was playing out an episode of *Law & Order.* And as much as he'd kept his gift for Elaina safe, he hadn't thought to put it in a box. The only thing separating the gift from a pair of scissors was the tissue it was wrapped in, and at this point, he wasn't sure where in the bag the gift was.

Duncan wondered if the other two people in the room could hear the silent screams of rage inside his head.

"Ya do see how ridiculous this is, don't you? *I* have no bag, no identification, because it's right there in front of you. *The arsehole* showed you his passport."

"His name's Stephen, actually," Kostas said, and Duncan's jaw clenched.

"I don't bloody care what his name is. Don't you find it the least bit odd he's not even arguing? That he's asking for legal aide?" Duncan stood and reached across the table toward Stephen's shirt collar. "It's my *bloody* wedding, for fuck's sake!"

Kostas was strong for the lanky git he was, wrenching Duncan's hand from the other guy's shirt.

"Please, Mr. McAllister. I don't want to write you up for assault as well."

Duncan slammed his hands down on the table, taking small pleasure in watching Stephen *and* Kostas flinch. Then he sat again.

He scrubbed a hand over his face, wincing as he touched his bruised cheek. He'd had everything planned perfectly, right down to his arriving with enough time to still have the entire day with both his and Elaina's families. And he had the perfect wedding gift for Elaina, one that would show her how much he loved her. He wasn't the best with words, but when he wanted to *show* her what she meant to him, he was a right genius, if he did say so himself. Asking for Elaina's hand in marriage more than a year before he proposed? Check. Learning enough Greek to properly ask her father for permission? Check again. Researching as much as he could about the ceremony of a Greek wedding to ensure the gift he presented to his wife spoke volumes as to how important she was to him—check. Almost. Because the item that said more than Duncan could articulate was not in his possession at the moment. It was being detained along with himself and the man who'd stolen it.

The door flew open, and Duncan had to do a double take to believe what he was seeing.

Kostas startled at the flurry of movement as Griffin and Noah strode into the room. The arse still sat with his arms calmly crossed over his chest. Hopefully, that was about to change.

"Good morning, everyone," Griffin said, a charming-as-shit grin plastered across his face. Noah just nodded at the three men in the room—the strong, silent partner. Duncan filled with hope. "I'm Griffin Reed, and this is my associate, Mr. Keating."

Duncan watched as Noah stifled a laugh, but Kostas didn't seem to catch it. He was eating this shite up. He shook Griffin's hand and then Noah's.

"I'm afraid you've inappropriately detained my client, Mr. McAllister."

Duncan's eyes widened, and Griffin gave him a little shrug. He was making this up as he went along, and it fucking seemed to be working.

"Mr. Reed, there was an altercation, and your…uh… client attacked this man and tried to steal—"

"Attacked?" Duncan kicked his chair out from behind him, and he was up again. "I should be phoning Scotland Yard—or whatever you call your police service here!"

"Hellenic Police," Kostas informed him, but Duncan just growled. That seemed to be his preferred form of speech today.

"Right. Enough already. I'm taking my bag, and I'm

walking out that door, ya daft knob. Ya don't even ken what you're doin.'"

Kostas held Duncan's bag in his hands and backed against the door, pushing it shut as he did.

"I'm sorry, but I can't let anyone leave until we've figured out who this belongs to."

"Did you tell him what was in it?" Noah asked.

"Nice one," Griffin said.

"Thanks, man," Noah remarked.

"I could name everything in the bag," Duncan said. "But the lock is busted. I swear it was our wedding date."

"Jesus, Duncan," Griffin said. "Did you try another date?"

Duncan turned to the wall behind him and punched it once. Then twice. He went for a third, but Noah caught his hand.

"I tried the date in reverse order," Duncan said. He squeezed his eyes shut and rubbed the back of his head, the two pills he'd swallowed doing nothing to ease the pain or clear his thoughts. He had to regain control, so he leaned against the wall, waiting for his breathing to slow, and tried to remember.

Shite. "I'm the daft knob," he mumbled. "I changed my mind. Last night when I bought the lock, my first thought was our wedding date, but then I got superstitious, aye. Using the wedding date before the wedding happened. That could be bad luck." He shook his head. Looked like bad luck came for him anyway. "So I switched it." He let out a long breath. "It's Elaina's birthday. Her bloody birthday, but my head is a mess, mates. I can't think straight."

Griffin took a step closer. "Hey, Duncan. Everything's going to be okay," he said.

"No," Duncan said louder, his voice firm. "It's not. Fuck, I never should have let go of the bag in the first place, but I was doing *exactly* what Elaina thinks I'm probably doing right now. I was freaking out."

Griffin put a palm on Duncan's shoulder, but nothing would soothe him.

"It just—it all hit me when I stepped off that plane and realized Scotland wasn't home anymore. And I—I couldn't catch my breath. I thought it was the jumper I was wearing, so I let go of the bag and took the fucking thing off."

All eyes were on Duncan, even the arse's. He could see the worry in his stare because Duncan was about to exonerate himself, but first he had to admit to *someone* why this had happened in the first place.

"I freaked out, mates. I fucking freaked out, and then this guy knocked me out cold, and since then everything is swimming in here." Duncan pointed to his head. "So I couldn't even think straight enough to remember the combination, tell A Levels over here that in the bag is a scarf trimmed in the McAllister red and green tartan, and then open the damn thing and show it to him. I could have been out of here more than an hour ago if I was bloody fucking conscious. Because the *only* thing that matters now is getting to Elaina."

Duncan removed the lock with the correct combination, and Kostas opened the bag and pulled out the scarf, nodding in recognition.

"You had this made for your wife? For the red scarf ritual?" he asked.

Duncan nodded. Of course he did. He was fine with having a traditional Greek wedding. It was important to Elaina, so that made it important to him. But aside from wearing his tartan on his kilt, he wanted to connect Elaina's Greek tradition with his own.

"I'm sorry, Mr. McAllister," he said. "You're free to go." He handed Duncan the tartan scarf, his phone, and the bag. Then he glanced at the other man at the table, the real assailant. "But I'm going to have to ask you to fill out a report and decide if you want to move forward with legal proceedings…"

Griffin motioned for the door, and Kostas stepped aside.

"You can email him the report. You've taken up enough of his time. Mr. McAllister has a wedding to get to."

Kostas nodded. "Of course, sir. *Thermá syncharitíria.* Congratulations. And my apologies…"

Duncan didn't wait to hear the rest. He pushed through the door as Griffin and Noah followed. He had a wedding to get to — and lots of explaining to do.

Chapter Eleven

GRIFFIN

Griffin sipped his champagne, which was tough because he wanted to drain his glass in one long gulp. Bullshit artist or not, he could have gotten them all in deeper trouble by trying to impersonate a litigator or whatever he was doing, yet somehow here they were.

Duncan leaned across the aisle and clinked his glass with Griffin's, then reached around to the seat in front of him and did the same with Noah. Then he threw back his bubbly like it was a shot of whisky.

"I thought you said you had a concussion," Griffin said. "Should you be, you know, drinking?"

Duncan waved a hand. "*Possible* concussion. I'd have to go to hospital to confirm, but"—he shook his empty champagne flute—"I'm feeling quite excellent right now. And, mates—that was simply brilliant. I mean, fucking brilliant."

Noah turned in his seat to face them.

"Which part? Us barging in on that bullshit episode of

Law and Order and helping you figure out your shit, or Reed snagging us a free upgrade to first class with his threat of litigation?"

"All of it," Duncan said. "The whole bloody day—well, since you two arrived. It was absolute shite before that, but now?" He raised his glass as a flight attendant walked by to offer him a refill. "Aye. This is how a day *should* begin for a man about to get married. It's all gonna work out, lads. I can feel it."

Duncan's smile fell.

"Then why aren't you smiling anymore?" Noah asked.

Duncan sighed. "Because maybe I *don't* feel it, but I'm trying to convince myself I do. I know Elaina loves me, but I think she's been waiting for me to grow up, to not be the guy who wakes up on the grass outside his flat because he was too drunk to find his key."

"That's not what happened today," Griffin said.

"Aye. But isn't this some version of it? Duncan McAllister getting himself into a right mess? I don't want to be a mess she has to clean up."

"You're not a mess," Griffin told him. "You're the guy who not only got the girl but got the girl's father to trust you enough to give you a really great job. Everything's fine now," he assured his friend, hoping he was telling the truth. "But you could have used my phone when I texted Maggie."

Duncan scrubbed a hand over his face, his fingers stopping to rest on the growing bruise beneath his eye. Then he shook his head.

"You told her I'm all right, yeah? That I'm on my way? I need to do the rest in person, face-to-face. Today was important," he said. "Almost more so than the wedding, what with our families meeting for the first time." Duncan laughed, but this wasn't the typical merriment Griffin remembered of his friend. This laugh sounded bitter, a harshness to Duncan's tone he hadn't heard before.

"Hey, man. She loves you. She said yes to marrying you. And today? Today wasn't your fault."

Duncan shrugged. "Wasn't it, though? I waited till the last minute for the tartan, got on the latest possible plane I could so I could stay in Aberdeen a bit longer. One day earlier, and this wouldn't have happened."

Noah shook his head. "You don't know that. There could have been a bigger asshole on yesterday's flight." All three of them chuckled, and Griffin could feel this interaction getting into dangerously emotional territory. "The way I see it," Noah added, "is that we're all fucking clueless. There's no rule book or manual for any of this. Best we can do is make up for the times we mess up by getting the big things right."

Duncan relaxed into his seat.

"Elaina, she'll be mad, aye," he told them. "She'll be mad, but if I get it all right from here on out, you're saying that will make up for it?"

Noah nodded.

Griffin wasn't so sure—not about Duncan, but about how each day he lied to Maggie, he was making a bigger and bigger mess. He swirled the pale gold liquid in his glass. He should be proud of what he'd done—getting them all on the flight back to Thessaloniki, *with* upgrades. But all it did was remind him that he'd been playing a part. Putting on a show. And he realized that's exactly what he was doing with Maggie. He could use her migraine as the excuse for not immediately thrusting the envelope in her face, but what about all those hours on the plane he had her undivided attention? He needed to say something, to get this off his chest and out into the open before it was too late.

"Oi, Griffin?" Duncan roused him from his thoughts. "My lad Noah says Elaina's going to forgive me. You're supposed to be helping me celebrate."

Griffin set the flute down and looked at Duncan, all his bravado for their Athens adventure having melted away.

"Maggie—she's okay, yeah?" Duncan asked.

Griffin nodded. "So this is, like, the sharing hour now?"

Duncan didn't say anything, just narrowed his eyes and waited.

"Fine," he said. Maybe he could stand to get a little advice from his friends. "I took a shot in the dark and won a fellowship with AmeriCorps, the place I work for now. It's extremely competitive, and I wasn't expecting to get it. I just wanted to see if I could, you know?" Both Duncan and Noah nodded. "But I got it. And now that it's mine, I want it. But if I accept, I have to move to D.C. for a year this fall."

Okay, so maybe he was supposed to say all of that to Maggie, but what the hell? A guy could only take so much, and even if this didn't solve his problem, it felt good to say out loud, to admit that he wanted this.

Duncan emptied his glass again. "See! This day is back on track. Good things for everyone!"

He clapped Griffin on the shoulder, but Griffin shook his head.

"Maggie doesn't know," he said.

"Why not?" Noah asked.

He took in a measured breath. It wasn't his place to tell them about Maggie's medical past, even if she survived a brain aneurysm and the surgery to remove it. God, she really was the strongest person he knew, so why couldn't he say to her what he just said to them?

"I don't know," he admitted, throwing his head back against his seat. Then he groaned. "Shit. I'm ruining your moment, Duncan. We're celebrating your freedom, right? I'm sorry, man. Maybe Keating has more wisdom to lighten the mood."

Noah averted his eyes and cleared his throat. Well shit,

Keating was hiding something, too.

"Out with it," Duncan said, nudging Noah's shoulder. "We're all getting in touch with our *feelings*, Keating. Your turn."

Noah pulled his messenger bag out from under the seat in front of him. He reached inside an inner pocket and retrieved a small velvet box.

"Well, bloody fucking hell," Duncan said under his breath.

A tiny weight lifted off Griffin's chest. He realized in his unfortunate encounter with him on their last flight how much Noah was willing to sacrifice for Jordan. He'd already let go of any mistrust he had for the guy. But this? This confirmed what an ass Griffin had been to ever doubt how much Noah cared for his friend, and for the first time since he'd left Maggie in Thessaloniki, he'd smiled and meant it. No pretense. No show. He was just damned happy for Jordan—and for Noah, too.

"Congratulations," he said, raising his glass.

"She still has to say yes," Noah said, but he raised his flute as well.

"Mates, we have turned this shite day around. Jordan is going to say yes. You and Maggie are going to figure out this fellowship thing, and Elaina is going to marry me—after she forgives me, of course."

If Duncan could turn a day like today around, then Griffin could get over whatever the hell was holding him back. He wasn't the guy he was before he met Maggie. He was the version of himself she made him want to be. And that meant laying all his cards on the table no matter what the outcome— even if one possible outcome could destroy him. He owed her his best self.

"*Slainte*," Griffin said.

"*Slainte*," Noah and Duncan repeated in unison.

And they drank to the women who would hopefully say yes; who would forgive and say *I do*; who would understand the paralysis of fear and still believe that chasing a dream meant nothing if it meant doing it without her.

Griffin thought about his first date with Maggie and their repurposing of UNO cards into a Truth or Dare kind of game—minus the dare. A WILD card meant the bearer could ask the other anything he or she wanted, big or small, and the question had to be answered with the complete and utter truth.

But Maggie shouldn't have to draw a card to get that from him. He needed to trust her, to offer it willingly, to give her everything.

Not just the WILD card. Griffin was going full deck. All in.

Chapter Twelve

"Are you sure you don't want to join us?" Maggie asked, and Miles made an exaggerated effort to examine his neatly trimmed fingernails.

"Manis and pedis, Mags? I mean, I *am* well-groomed, but I draw the line at spending money for someone else to do what I can do for myself."

She shrugged. "I'm just flattered the bridal party invited me along. Plus, it's Elaina's cousin, so it won't cost much."

"So there's still going to be a wedding?" he asked as Jordan strode up behind Maggie.

"I don't know," Jordan said. "Elaina is *pissed*. I told her the guys found Duncan and are bringing him back. Noah said he wasn't ditching her, that he'd actually been hurt and detained and was afraid to tell her about it in a text. They were rushing to get their flights figured out. But no matter what I say to her, she just gets angrier."

"Why?" Maggie asked.

"Because Duncan called Griffin instead of her. Look, all I know is she's going through with everything that was on the docket for today. And if Duncan shows up...I mean *when* he shows up..." Jordan hesitated, winding a lock of hair around her finger until the tip turned white.

"Whoa," Miles started, watching Jordan fidget where she stood. "I'm sensing I'm about to get more drama than I bargained for."

Maggie backhanded him on the shoulder.

"What?" he said with a laugh. "I'm just glad the spotlight's off of me."

"It's okay," Jordan said. "He's right. I am being a little dramatic. It's just...Duncan and Elaina? They're the ones who got it right from the start, you know? *Zero* drama. He liked her. She pretended for maybe five minutes not to like him, and then *bam.* Perfect couple. And now?" She shrugged. "They're going to be fine, right? If he was never thinking of bailing, then they're still the model couple."

Miles nodded to Maggie, but he wasn't smiling anymore. "This is why I keep my distance, Mags." Then he turned to Jordan. "Look, I'm sorry if I seem like an insensitive asshole, but I'm good without the whole mani-pedi thing, and I'm good without"—he waved his hand in the air—"the drama of *will they or won't they*."

Miles kissed Maggie on the cheek and backed toward the rear of the restaurant.

"I'm gonna go walk on the beach." *Clear my head.*

Maggie glanced out the window and then back at him. "It's not as warm as it looks out there. I think the taxi driver said it was just below forty degrees."

Miles zipped his black leather jacket over his hoodie, then winked at her and grinned.

"I know people who've hitchhiked in worse."

She rolled her eyes, and that was enough to convince him

she wouldn't push him to share what the hell was up his ass—
because, honestly, he wasn't 100 percent sure. He was just...
off.

So what if somewhere in this city was a guy who'd driven
him crazy in an airplane bathroom? Somewhere in this
city—right. Like Miles had the city to hide him. Come this
evening, Alex would probably be working the party. What
were the odds that a restaurant's sous chef was *not* working
the owner's own daughter's wedding? When he'd walked into
that bathroom with a stranger, he expected to part just the
same. But something happened in that confined space, in that
miniature pocket of time, and it wasn't about the foreplay that
almost was.

He watched as Jordan pulled Maggie toward the group
of women who were converting part of the restaurant into a
miniature salon. Then he exited to what was, for the season,
an unused patio.

The wind was brisk, but the cold air felt good. It felt like
freedom.

He threw up his hood and headed toward the water.

He breathed in the salty air, making it close enough to the
shore for a fine mist to spray his cheeks.

"You *are* a grade-A asshole," he told himself. But *that?*
He glanced back toward the restaurant. *That* was why he
was no good at weddings. Watching two people pledge
their lives to each other made him long for something he'd
convinced himself a long time ago wasn't in the cards for
him. And watching an almost-couple like Duncan and Elaina
almost not make it? All it did was remind him that wanting
something and holding onto it were mutually exclusive. He'd
experienced that firsthand. So he taught himself not to want
anything more than fun, and that was working out pretty well
for him. Did he want Duncan and Elaina to crash and burn?
Of course not. Did he see that as more of a possibility than

Maggie and Jordan did? Sure. But he didn't need to spread his jadedness all over their hope for a happy ending.

After a few deep breaths, he turned to walk a stretch of the hotel-lined beach. Short white buildings bordered the sand, and even in the cool weather there were tourists enjoying coffee on a balcony and a couple a few yards off removing their shoes to dip their toes in the surf.

He jumped back as a wave rolled in, coming closer than the rest. Then he laughed at himself for being afraid of the consequences of making contact with the water. What did that say about his emotional state? He could write his doctoral thesis analyzing it, but with only five months to go in his program, it probably wasn't wise to change topics now.

He checked his phone. There were a few hours before he had to get ready for the rehearsal dinner—provided it was still happening. He'd run inside and make sure Maggie was cool with him taking off for a bit, and then? He'd just walk.

As he started to hike back up to the patio, he spotted a figure leaning against the restaurant's concrete ivory facade. The guy stood with one leg crossed over the other and his arms folded in front of his chest. After nodding in Miles's direction, the man took a drag from the cigarette dangling from his lips and then reached for it with his right hand. He waited to speak until Miles was in earshot.

"Did you know?" Alex asked, an almost-smile playing at his lips. "You weren't surprised when I told you my name in the airport. Did you know who I was?"

Miles played with the idea of a lie, but that wasn't him. No matter what came of this situation, he was nothing if not upfront.

He retrieved Alex's business card from his pocket and held it up for him to see.

Alex nodded slowly. "So why not tell me? You sat there the rest of the flight pretending you didn't know this might happen."

That was a legitimate question. But what was he going to do? Tell this stranger that kissing him in an airplane bathroom felt anything *but* strange? That he'd let his guard down long enough to wonder what it would be like to kiss this man again only because he'd thought he was safe from that ever happening. And now here he was, staring at those lips again, wanting what he shouldn't want.

"It's complicated," was all he said, and he rolled his eyes at himself. God, he hated that word, hated that he'd become the kind of guy who used it as an excuse to shut down.

Alex took a long, slow drag of the cigarette, then turned his head to the side to exhale.

"We were on a fucking plane, Miles. Strangers on a goddamned plane. We could have had a nice chat about what I do, about how you know the Tripoli family. It's just talking," Alex said. "You sat there the whole time knowing who I was, knowing my name…"

Miles studied his own shoes before looking at him again.

"I know," he said. "I'm just— I liked you. I like you now. And I don't want to." He scratched the back of his neck. "Liking a stranger is one thing. We meet. We make out. We never see each other again. And I may wonder, *What if?* But there's nothing I can do about it. But knowing your name and that I might bump into you again? That changed the game."

That almost-smile that threatened to undo Miles on the spot disappeared completely.

"I'm not playing a game, Miles." Alex shook his head. "You're a piece of work," he added. "So sorry for your predicament."

Jesus, he was doing this all wrong. But something about this guy made him do ridiculous things like say exactly what he was thinking and want to press him up against the building and kiss him again.

Alex straightened, took another drag, and then pushed off the wall.

"*Vlakas*," he said. "You knew we'd see each other. We could have made a fun weekend of it, no expectations. But since things are so complicated, I'll leave you to your brooding on the beach. I've met enough guys like you, Miles. I don't need complicated, either." Alex strode off around the side of the building.

Miles wasn't the type to chase after anyone. But he found himself following Alex, telling himself it was for no other reason than to clear the air, if only to avoid Alex sneezing in his soup later that night. It had nothing to do with those lips, the ones he could still taste if he closed his eyes.

"Hey, Alex. Wait a minute. I didn't mean I was playing games with you."

Alex extinguished the cigarette on the side of the building and tossed it in one of the many trash bins that hid behind a short wall next to a door.

"Are you here to complicate things?" Alex asked, shaking his head as his lips parted in a smile. Then he laughed, a genuine laugh, and for a second Miles forgot what he came here to say. All he wanted was that smile to stay right where it was and for those full lips to take his again.

Fucking focus, Miles.

"No," he said. "Maybe. I don't know what *vlakas* means, but I'm sure I deserved it. I guess I just wanted to say that I'm usually much better at *not* being complicated."

"I don't know you," Alex started. "I don't know what you deserve. *Vlakas*—stupid—that was for *me*." He paused. "Because I liked you, too." He ran a hand through his thick, sandy hair, and Miles clenched his fists at his sides, willing them *not* to relive the feeling of those locks against his own skin.

Seriously, Miles. Do not let one stranger throw you off your game. Not that it's a game. Shit. He was already in over his head, which was brand-new territory, considering how safe he'd been playing it for years.

"It's not as if I asked you to marry me in an airplane toilet."

Miles chuckled. He didn't mean to, but the thought made him wonder how many proposals *did* happen in such a location.

"I know," Miles said. "But—"

Alex shook his head, cutting him off. "Or move in with me," he added. "What gives you the right to think I expected any more from what happened than you did?"

Okay, Miles thought. *Now you're a grade-A asshole.* Because Alex was right. He hadn't asked Miles for anything other than a few minutes of fun. Miles hadn't withheld the truth about knowing who he was because of Alex's expectations. He'd done it because he was terrified of his own.

"Why don't you have an accent?" he asked.

"What?" Alex's dark brows pulled together, and Miles took small pleasure in catching him off guard.

"I could tell you weren't American," he said. "But your accent is so slight, I wasn't sure you were Greek until you translated for that woman on the plane."

Alex pulled a key from his pocket and unlocked the door next to him, pausing in the frame before stepping into what Miles could see was the restaurant's kitchen.

Miles stepped inside after him.

"What are you doing?" Alex asked, the corners of his mouth curling up again.

Miles shrugged. "I'm *not* expecting a proposal—or for you to ask me to move in with you. But it seems a shame for us to profess our *like* for each other and then walk away."

Alex nodded and backed farther into the kitchen.

"My father is Greek, my mother American. They never

married. He lives here, and she lives in New York. After spending my summers in the U.S., I decided to stay for university. Hence the accent—or lack thereof."

Alex took one more step back, then turned and walked farther into the building. He left the door open.

This was an invitation. For what, though? Miles wasn't about to ask. He wasn't going to overthink. He was just going to accept.

He turned back to the door and pulled it closed behind him.

Chapter Thirteen

MAGGIE

Maggie examined her cherry red nails, a bold contrast from their usual unpolished state. She smiled at the hustle and bustle around her. Despite the way the day had started, the bride was enjoying herself. There was a hopefulness in the air Maggie hadn't felt only an hour before, and she couldn't help but get caught up in it all, in what it meant to be here with Griffin—in how far they'd come the past year. This trip would be proof that she could step out of her comfort zone without any major issues. She had feared exhaustion or worse—a migraine—after the long trip, but she'd slept so well on the plane she wasn't sure she was even jet-lagged. And even with Miles off being moody on the beach, she was okay. Jordan treated her like they'd been friends for years, and Maggie took satisfaction in knowing she could shake up her world a bit and still be okay.

Ambrosia was closed for the weekend for wedding festivities, but that didn't mean the kitchen wasn't running at full force. As each girl finished getting her nails done, she was escorted to another corner of the restaurant where a table was covered with Greek delicacies. Maggie snacked on grilled vegetables with *tzatziki*, unable to suppress her grin with each bite. If she had to wait for Jordan to finish her manicure, she couldn't think of a better way to do it. While some of Elaina's relatives spoke English, the conversation around her was all in Greek, so Maggie smiled and nodded whenever someone looked in her direction, but she was happy for the respite amid all of the commotion.

Her phone buzzed on the table next to her, and her heart leaped. She hadn't realized until then how much she wished Griffin were there to experience this morning of firsts with her—first time away from Minneapolis since she'd been on her own again, first time out of the country, first time thinking she wouldn't always be afraid of more firsts. But when she looked at her screen, she found it was only Miles.

Miles: *You doing okay?*

Maggie: *Yeah, you? Hey, where are you?*

While she was grateful to Miles for joining them on the trip, the whole wedding thing seemed to have him bent out of shape. And in the four years she'd known him, Miles Parker was never one to be ruffled by anyone or anything.

Miles: *I'm getting a tour of the kitchen.*

Maggie: *Please explain.*

Miles: **sigh* Remember the guy from the plane?*

Maggie: *You mean the guy who visibly rocked your*

socks at the gate? Yeah. I think we all remember.

Miles: *Alex. He's sort of the sous chef at Ambrosia.*

Maggie let out a small giggle, thinking, *See? This day is so going to end up better than it started.*

Maggie: *No further explanation needed. Enjoy yourself.*

Miles: *You sure you're okay without me?*

She took a selfie, holding up a manicured hand for him to see and making sure she captured the table of food behind her. Then she pressed *send*.

Miles: *Looks like you are being very well taken care of.*

Maggie: *And I'm drinking Turkish coffee. Holy caffeine. I may be up for days.*

Miles: *I'll see you soon, then?*

Maggie: *No rush. Enjoy yourself.*

Miles: *I think I will.*

Jordan plopped down in the seat next to her. "Griffin?"

Maggie shook her head. "Miles. Remember the guy from the plane, or after the plane, I should say?"

Jordan giggled. "Uh, I don't think any of us will forget witnessing a kiss like that."

"Well," Maggie continued. "Looks like he's the one in the

kitchen making all of this amazing food."

"Get out!" Jordan's eyes widened. "Maybe this is a sign, you know? Like, everyone will get a happy ending, even Miles!" She sighed. "The guys will land, get Duncan here, and everything will be fine, right? This whole wedding thing has to happen."

Maggie smiled and took a sip of her coffee. She couldn't explain it—her unwavering confidence—but she knew there was no way they'd leave Greece without seeing a wedding.

"It's going to happen," she said.

Jordan looked at Maggie's small coffee mug and wrinkled her nose.

"Elaina tried for a full year to get me to drink her coffee, but I never did."

Maggie swirled the remnants of the liquid in her cup before polishing it off. "It's really good," she said. "Strong, but good."

"And she is going to try it now." Elaina strode up behind Jordan's chair, placing her hands on her friend's shoulders. Jordan swallowed hard, and Maggie laughed.

"Oh my goodness," Maggie said. "It's just coffee."

Elaina bent, draping her arms over Jordan's shoulders and resting her chin on her head.

"But this one is a pussy lightweight," Elaina informed her. "She cannot handle her liquor, which means she probably cannot handle her coffee."

Maggie laughed. Jordan's lips pursed into a pout.

"Why is everyone ganging up on me for my beverage intake?" She raised her brows in Elaina's direction. "I'd expect it from this one, but you, too, Maggie?"

Maggie laughed, and Elaina kissed Jordan on the cheek before straightening up again.

"Papa?" Elaina's father was at the other end of the table replenishing an almost empty tray.

He looked up, and his eyes shone when he gazed at his daughter. "What do you need, *koritsi mou*?"

Maggie let out a wistful sigh. The closest thing to a father she ever had was her grandpa. But he was gone now, and Gran was in Florida. She realized that her immediate family consisted of Miles and Griffin, and the thought both terrified and delighted her.

"More coffee, *se parakalo*? For Jordan."

Jordan rolled her eyes, and all three of them laughed.

"Fine," Jordan relented. "Only because it's *your* day, all right? Then I'm off the hook?"

Elaina's father darted back into the kitchen and came out moments later with a small cup on a saucer. He set it down on the table in front of Jordan, and Maggie peered into it with her. Despite the shallow depth of the mug, the coffee was so dark they couldn't see the bottom.

"You got this," Maggie assured her. "It's just coffee. Really thick, really strong, unsweetened coffee."

Jordan rolled her eyes. "You aren't helping."

While Jordan contemplated her coffee, Elaina pulled her cell phone from her pocket and stared at it. She held it out for Maggie and Jordan to see.

"Why do you think this is all I got?"

Maggie read the short message.

Duncan: *Forgive me. I couldn't get on the second plane.*

"Maybe his phone died," Maggie offered.

Elaina sighed. "Griffin has a phone, no? And Noah, too? Why do they send all the messages and Duncan says nothing?"

Jordan opened her mouth to say something, but Elaina waved her off.

"I scare him," Elaina said softly.

"You don't scare him," Jordan said, and Elaina gave her a pointed look. "Okay, you might be a little scary, but it's part of your charm."

"Do you think he is marrying me because he is afraid not to after all of this time? Noah did say in his text that he was afraid to tell me what happened."

Maggie and Jordan both shook their heads. Maggie didn't know Elaina and Duncan other than the one time she'd met them last year and from what she'd learned from Griffin. Elaina was guarded, yes. And maybe a little rough around the edges. But Duncan wore his heart on his sleeve, and she'd known the minute she met them that he was over the moon for this girl.

"Elaina," Jordan started, grabbing her friend's hand, but Elaina just shook her head and took a shaky breath.

"I don't want him to feel forced to do something that doesn't feel right to him. I don't want to scare him into staying." She took Jordan's coffee from the table. "And I will not force you to drink the stupid coffee," Elaina said. "I will not force anyone to do anything."

And with that Elaina retreated from the restaurant and up the stairs that led to the Tripoli family's apartment.

Maggie looked at her phone, opening up the last text Griffin had sent her. She'd seen it pop up when she was getting her nails done but couldn't read it. She only now remembered it was there.

Griffin: *We've got Duncan. Catching an afternoon flight back. The first one available. We need to talk, okay? As soon as I see you. There's something I should have told you before we left, and I don't want to wait anymore. I hope you'll forgive me for waiting this long.*

"What?"

"What?" Jordan asked, and Maggie realized she'd spoken out loud.

"Huh?" Maggie asked. "I mean, nothing. It's nothing." Because as comfortable as she had felt in her recent surroundings, Jordan wasn't *her* friend. She wasn't a person Maggie confided in. That person was Griffin, and if it couldn't be Griffin, it was Miles. Well, how could she confide in Griffin about a frighteningly cryptic text that he had sent? And how could she confide in Miles when he was probably having sex in much too close a vicinity to the evening's meal preparations?

"Are you sure?" Jordan asked. "I was about to go talk to Elaina, but if you need someone…"

Maggie waved her off. "No, no. Go talk to Elaina. I'm sure there's a perfectly good explanation why Duncan hasn't called her yet. She needs a friend right now, and you can smooth things over."

Jordan bounced on her toes. "Okay. I'll be back soon."

And she was off and up the stairs, leaving Maggie to read Griffin's text over and over again.

She had tried not to notice it, how something with Griffin had been off the past couple days. Now she couldn't help but see the signs. Whenever she'd seen that look in his eyes, that silent retreat, she'd asked if everything was okay.

"Totally fine, Pippi," was his go-to answer, and she'd trusted him. He was always quick to cut off conversation about anything other than the mundane with a kiss, and she hadn't questioned it because who would question kissing that man, especially when just his kiss could drive her nearly insane? If something was up, he would tell her, right?

But something *was* up, and he'd waited until now to tell her. What if this whole thing with Duncan and Elaina was giving him second thoughts about their relationship? What if he'd been afraid to tell her before the trip? Breaking bad news to her while she was so far from home—so far from safety—wasn't even the worst of it. The worst of it was that after a promise to always, *always* lay their cards out on the table, Griffin had been holding back.

She looked around the crowded room, at the friends and family of the bride and groom—Duncan's relatives included—laughing and enjoying one another's company. She thought about Miles with Alex, and Griffin on a plane—and all the hope that had filled her evaporated as quickly as it had come.

In a sea of people, Maggie felt utterly alone.

Chapter Fourteen

It wasn't as if Miles was a stranger to a kitchen. He worked in one, too. He was just better versed in beverages, pastries, and the occasional panini than he was in full gourmet meals.

Alex dried his hands after giving them a good scrub in the sink and then busied himself juicing lemons and cracking eggs into a bowl at a stainless-steel island. Miles strolled toward him, observing his surroundings as if they were exhibits in the Louvre.

"You don't have to be afraid of touching anything," Alex said, side-eyeing him from where he beat the lemons and eggs together. He poured the mixture into a large pot, giving whatever else was in there with it a few lazy stirs.

Miles released his hands from the front pocket of his jeans and inched closer, a finger poised to taste.

"After you wash," Alex said, stopping him short, and Miles bit back a smile.

He unzipped his jacket. "Where should I..."

"There's a closet over there." Alex nodded to a small alcove off to his left, just past what looked like a walk-in cooler. Miles followed his gaze and rid himself of both his jacket and hoodie, leaving him in only his T-shirt and jeans.

"There are clean aprons on the other side," Alex continued, and because his back was still to him, Miles let himself smile this time. He could tell from Alex's tone—not a command yet not nearly playful—that he wasn't out of the woods yet. But this wasn't just some quick tour and *see ya later.* Alex was asking him to stay, and by pulling the crisp white cotton from the hanger, Miles was accepting the invitation.

He ambled to the sink first, cleansing his hands like he was a surgeon, soaping up to his elbows and rinsing with water hot enough to turn his skin pink. When he finished, he used the same towel he saw Alex use to dry off.

Alex was juicing another lemon, the rind of the fruit in his palm as he pressed it over the raised peak of the appliance. He wore a short-sleeved black chef's jacket over dark jeans, the muscles in his forearms tensing as he wrung the lemon to nothing but pulp.

"Didn't know you smoked," Miles started, then rolled his eyes at himself. Judgmental was so not his usual M.O., but then again, nothing about today was *usual.* For the guy who put fun above all else, he sure was doing a bang-up job of making this encounter everything but. Self-sabotage also wasn't his way, but there were these…*feelings*…seeping out from the places he had buried them, and they were making him do and say things so utterly unlike him. It would take everything in his power to turn off his psychoanalytical tendencies and to just *be.* Three days. He could handle being in the vicinity of this man for three days before escaping back to Minnesota's sub-zero temps and its complete and utter un-Greeceness.

Alex kept his eyes on the other half of the lemon he was pulverizing, a ghost of a smile tugging at his lips.

"I don't smoke. Not habitually." He ground the rind into the juicer, even after nothing was left to juice. "But when I need to clear my head?" He shrugged. "We all have vices. Mine is the occasional *tsigaro*."

Miles pressed his hands flat atop the steel island, letting out a long sigh, and Alex finally looked up.

"What?" he asked, and Miles shook his head.

"I don't like that you just made the word 'cigarette' sound sexy."

Alex grinned. "You seem not to like a lot of things when it comes to me, including *me*."

Miles shook his head. "You're twisting my words," he told him. "I said I didn't *want* to like you."

But he did. Every second he was in Alex's presence, that feeling he didn't want to have, it only grew stronger.

Alex turned back to what he was doing and added the juice he'd just squeezed into the steaming pot on the stove. But he was smiling as he did.

Miles watched the tendons in Alex's neck tighten and release, and he allowed himself a self-satisfied grin. This guy may have gotten to him, but shit if Miles hadn't gotten to Alex, too. So what now?

"Can I help?" he asked.

Alex nodded. "Come stir."

He approached with caution, relaxing when he saw the tension leave Alex's shoulders.

"Egg lemon soup. It needs to mix in and heat through," he said. "Then we will chill it until the reception tomorrow."

Alex grabbed Miles's hand and placed it around the wand of the spoon. "Just like that—long, slow circles. *Entaxei*?"

Miles furrowed his brow.

"Sorry," Alex said, letting go of the spoon and leaving it to his assistant. "It means *okay*. When I'm here, in Greece, I slip back into the language."

"It's nice," Miles admitted. "The words—even when you're angry—I like the sound of them coming from your lips."

He could flirt comfortably now. Both men had admitted their attraction and that there were zero expectations from either of them. So why not see where the rest of the day went? Sure, there was a part of him that knew he was approaching dangerous territory, but didn't he enjoy a little risk, especially when there was the safety net of a flight back to the States at the end of the weekend? "Does it happen in the States, too? The Greek and English together?"

Alex shook his head. "When I'm here I speak only Greek. But you"—he nodded toward the interior of the restaurant— "and all the Scots and the other Americans? It puts my head in two different places. Does that make sense?"

Yeah. Miles knew the feeling of being in two head spaces at once, the duality of wanting to both lay this guy out on that stainless-steel island and then walk away without a second thought, safe and secure, while also wanting this beautiful man to keep talking, keep revealing himself even though every word Alex spoke brought Miles closer to the danger zone. To caring. To wondering about possibilities beyond this weekend.

But he wasn't about to say any of that, so he just kept it simple.

"It makes sense."

Miles concentrated on the rhythm of the spoon moving against the thick soup, the savory aroma making his mouth water. Alex left him to it and backed away toward the cooler, unbuttoning the chef's shirt to reveal a fitted white tank top underneath.

"Thanks for your help," Alex said. "That was the last thing I had to prepare before this evening, so I'm going to take off."

Miles's eyes widened, and Alex barked out a laugh, the tank rising from his jeans and revealing a dark trail that Miles wanted to follow—just after he told this guy to fuck off.

"I'm sorry," Alex said. "I'm an asshole, but I have to say… it was worth it."

Miles wanted to fling a spoonful of whatever this soup was at that smug grin on Alex's face, but the liquid was hot enough to burn, and he couldn't justify scarring that face, even if it was mocking him. Instead he scraped the spoon clean and laid it on the island, brushing off his hand on his still-pristine apron.

"Did you even need me to stir?" he asked, and Alex shook his head.

"Just once or twice. The heat's already turned down so the soup can cool."

Maybe Miles deserved a little teasing, but he was done holding back. He stalked toward Alex, who didn't flinch at his approach. Fuck. He welcomed it. Miles cupped his face in his hands but kept his momentum until the two of them slammed up against the cooler door.

"Are we even now?" Miles asked, using every ounce of restraint to keep his mouth from crashing onto the one that was half a breath away.

Alex chuckled, unfazed. "Ask me when the weekend's done," he said, and there it was. A challenge.

Miles froze, his whole alpha thing backfiring, as he was clearly the one who was fazed.

"You don't look like the tourist type," Alex continued. "And I'm willing to bet you're on the first plane back to the States as soon as the wedding's over."

"So?" he asked, wanting to call his bluff, yet he knew already this was not the kind of guy who backed down.

"So stay with me this weekend. I know you are here with your friends, but when you aren't with them—be with me."

It wasn't a command. It wasn't a plea.

It was three little words that simply made sense.

"Okay," Miles said.

And with that he let it all go—the repressed emotion, the defense mechanisms, the hesitation—all of it. He let it fucking go.

Then he kissed the man who asked for nothing but three days. Three days and his name.

"It's nice to meet you, Alex," Miles said in between flicks of his tongue against lips he'd been hungry for since the airport.

Alex wrapped his arms around Miles's waist, tugging him closer as he parted his lips in a smile.

"It's nice to meet you, too, Miles."

Chapter Fifteen

Jordan sprawled like a starfish on the hotel bed, luxuriating in the softness of the hotel robe. She missed Noah. Of course she did. But this alone time—quiet time without a story to write or a paper to grade; without Elaina putting on a false smile for all her guests, lying to Duncan's family and her own that his flight was delayed; without worrying about the money Noah just spent on a round-trip ticket to Athens to rescue Duncan from whatever mess he'd gotten himself into—yes, this alone time was *good*.

The weekend would fly by, and then she and Noah would be traveling to the U.K. and taking a train to Scotland, back to the scene of the crime, so to speak. She laughed quietly to herself, picturing the vestibule on the train where Noah had first kissed her. A stranger in a strange place, he'd been exactly what she needed to interrupt her carefully planned life. Okay, so he'd traveled to Aberdeen with his ex-girlfriend, which led to her dating Griffin early in the semester. Maybe things weren't exactly smooth sailing after that first kiss, but it was the start of something that would eventually alter her life.

I'm not *a spontaneous guy*, he'd told her that first summer when they'd traveled Europe before going home to spend their first real year as a couple in two different states. *But you make me want to step outside that safe zone, even if there's risk. Because despite the occasional mess—and the scars we have to prove it—loving you is worth all of it.*

Jordan rubbed a finger over the scar on her forehead, caused by an unfortunate turn of events that included alcohol, mistletoe, and the edge of a pub table greeting her as she fell. She imagined the one on Noah's palm, when she'd accidentally barreled into him after their British Novel in Film class and he'd cut it on a broken bottle.

Sure, what people saw were scars, but what Jordan saw were reminders that despite the hurt and the work, what she had with Noah was worth all of it. She hoped Duncan could do that for Elaina, show her that whatever happened today was just one of those wounds that would heal and scar and remind them that they are stronger together no matter what life throws at them.

With that comforting thought, she closed her eyes, barely letting herself drift off when there was a quiet knock on the door.

She leapt from the bed.

"Noah?" she asked, giddy at the thought of his return. Okay, so maybe the alone time wasn't as great as she thought.

But when she looked through the peephole, Jordan saw a fidgeting Maggie. Her heart sank. Had it been selfish of her to want time alone in her room? After all of the people and the food and the noise and—ugh. She just needed some quiet. But Maggie was here all by herself, not even Miles to provide the buffer she probably needed.

"Maggie!" Jordan said as she threw the door open. "Hey.

Everything okay?"

Maggie stood before her in a casual yet elegant navy dress with white polka dots. Her tangerine waves cascaded over her shoulders and onto her bare arms. She was a beautiful girl, and it warmed Jordan's heart to see how she lit up when she was with Griffin and how he did the same with her.

Maggie's features relaxed into a warm smile.

"Sorry," she said. "I can't relax, and when I can't relax, I look for things to do, and I know we still have another hour until we need to be back at the restaurant, but the only thing I had to keep me busy was to get ready. So I'm ready. But…I can't zip my dress. Would you mind?"

Maggie spun so her back was to Jordan, who had the dress zipped in seconds.

"Thanks," she said. "I'll see you soon." She turned to head back to her room. Was it really only an hour before dinner?

"Maggie, wait."

Maggie stopped to face her again.

"Are you worried that they aren't back yet?" Jordan asked her.

The other girl let out a long breath, and Jordan realized they'd both been worrying, only separately. It was time to commiserate.

"Come on in," she told her, and Maggie followed her into the room, taking a seat in the desk chair. "I'm sorry."

"For what?"

"That I let us spend the afternoon worrying about this on our own. Griffin would kill me if he knew I left you hanging like that."

Maggie laughed. "I appreciate the thought," she said. "But I'm pretty capable of taking care of myself. I know when we met in Chicago I was not at my best, but…"

Jordan shook her head. *Shit.* She was out of practice with the whole friend-making thing. She hadn't forgotten meeting in Chicago last year when Griffin brought Maggie to the Aberdeen reunion. Maggie had joined them for glass after glass of champagne even though the alcohol and subsequent dehydration triggered a headache that laid her out for the rest of the evening.

"I didn't mean to insinuate you weren't okay on your own," she told Maggie. "I'm sorry. Ugh, can we maybe just start over from when you knocked on my door? I'll do better this time." She chewed on her top lip, and Maggie smiled.

"We're good. No worries. Besides…if Griffin wants to kill anyone, it'll be Miles. He's technically my chaperone, though I hope it's obvious I'm doing fine without him."

Jordan wanted to laugh off the comment, but Maggie's nonchalance felt too forced, so she decided to try again.

"What else are you worried about?" Jordan asked, sitting on the edge of her bed.

"I'm not," Maggie insisted, but Jordan wasn't buying it.

"Okay," Jordan said. "I just need to dry my hair and throw on my dress. Give me ten minutes. Then we'll head to Ambrosia a little early for a coffee and a chat. What do you think?"

Maggie nodded and stood up. "Okay. Deal. I'll go grab my coat."

Chapter Sixteen

Maggie

The hotel was only a few buildings down the road from Ambrosia, so the girls walked in silence for the few minutes it took to get there. They entered the restaurant and were immediately ushered by one of Elaina's relatives—Maggie thought maybe an uncle, though she couldn't remember his name—to the *small* party room that would house this evening's festivities.

"This is the small room?" Maggie asked, and Jordan giggled as they both handed their coats to a server.

"I think they're using the whole main restaurant for the wedding, so yeah. This counts as small," Jordan said.

Maggie spun slowly, taking in the surroundings—a long row of pillow-topped booth seats lined the side wall, each with a rectangular table and two chairs facing the booth. The windowed wall that looked out over the beach housed seven round tables, each seating four. Small, recessed lights gave the earth-toned furniture a warm, amber glow.

Much like this morning's display of food, there was a table at the far end set with appetizers and shots of what she was sure was ouzo.

"Okay," Jordan said as they approached the table. "I don't see coffee."

Maggie picked up a shot first. "When in Rome? Or Greece, I guess."

Jordan's eyes widened, and Maggie could tell the girl was trying not to say the wrong thing, so she let her off the hook as quickly as she could.

"That weekend in Chicago—I knew my limits, and I ignored them. I don't know how much Griffin's told you, but I had an aneurysm at nineteen." Maggie let out a bitter laugh. "I had a great surgeon. Saved my life, but I'm not…the same."

"Oh, Maggie," Jordan said. "No, I didn't know. I mean, I knew something was up that weekend, but I had no idea…"

Maggie had never asked Griffin not to say anything, but at the same time her heart swelled to know he hadn't, that he'd left it as *her* story to tell, if she wanted to.

"It's okay," Maggie said, even though her voice shook a little on those words. Going back over what happened was never easy because it always brought that fear of *what if it happens again* to the surface. "I'm not the same," she continued. "But I'm getting better. I'm learning to be okay with what I can't change. But that weekend? Griffin didn't know the history—why I got the headaches and couldn't drink like most college students did. I didn't want him to think I was different or fragile or someone he needed to take care of, so I was reckless because I was scared." But Maggie wasn't on the blood thinners anymore. And yes, the migraines were still a regular part of her life, but she'd had three years to read her body's signals and anticipate her triggers—though they still snuck up on her from time to time. She couldn't control everything. A drink every now and then? She could do that.

She'd stayed hydrated on the flight. She'd slept. And aside from letting her worry get the best of her today, she felt great.

Miles wasn't here, Griffin wasn't here, and she was in a strange place all by herself—and she felt *great*.

"Oh my God," Maggie said and started giggling. Then laughing. And she hadn't even had the shot yet. "I'm *okay*."

She picked up another shot and handed it to the still-confused Jordan.

"All day I've been worried not just about this wedding and whether or not it would happen," she started, "but about Griffin and me—waiting for the other shoe to drop when I don't even think the first one ever did, you know?"

She expected Jordan to maintain that bug-eyed expression, to think her as crazy as she probably sounded, but instead she nodded.

"Holy shit," Jordan said. "It's like you just explained my mental state for the past two years, let alone today. Can I say again how sorry I am we didn't connect this afternoon before you came to my door?"

It didn't matter now. Maggie knew that no matter what happened from here on out, she'd be okay. She'd planned on this trip being an upset to her carefully laid out routine. She hadn't anticipated losing Griffin and Miles for the day, and that *had* thrown her for a loop. But she was still standing... with a full shot of ouzo in her hand, and dammit if she wasn't doing just fine.

"What are you two pussy lightweights waiting for?"

Elaina was next to them now, shot in hand. She was exquisite in an ice-blue toga-style gown with her black hair pulled back in an elegant bun with a few escaping tendrils framing her face.

"You're gorgeous," Maggie said, and Elaina rolled her eyes.

"I know it is cliché to wear something that looks like it

came from Aphrodite's closet, but I have fantastic shoulders. Duncan needs to see exactly what he is giving up." She eyed the two Americans still holding their shots. "Now yell *fuck it* or *opa* or something, and let's get on with it."

"Do I slam my shot glass on the ground when I'm done?" Jordan asked, and Maggie wasn't sure if she was messing with Elaina or if it was in earnest.

"Oooopa! Fuck it!" Elaina yelled, loud enough to turn heads, and she threw back the shot, then placed the empty glass back on the table.

Jordan shrugged and looked at Maggie. "I guess we don't shatter the glass."

"Opa!" Maggie yelled.

"Fuck it!" Jordan added.

And the two girls drank in unison, following Elaina's lead by salvaging the glasses.

Maggie's throat burned, and her head swam. In the past year she'd had the occasional beer or glass of white wine, but ouzo was a far cry from a drink she sipped slowly over the course of an entire evening.

"Shit," Maggie said, placing her hand on the corner of the table to steady her stance.

"Shit is right," Jordan said, and then let out a small hiccup followed by a giggle.

"Fucking shit," Elaina said, but her gaze moved past Maggie and Jordan to the room's open doorway. In it stood three men, visibly weary with travel, one of them with a noticeable bruise on his cheek and his eye swollen half shut.

Griffin and Noah froze, waiting for Duncan to make the first move. When his eyes landed on Elaina, he took a small step back. A stagger, Maggie thought. And she knew Elaina had accomplished what she set out to do. If, in fact, Duncan had gotten cold feet, the way he looked at Elaina now spoke volumes. He knew what he was missing.

But as he barreled through the growing crowd of people, some of them surely his own family who tried to pull him aside, Maggie knew that stagger wasn't out of realization for what he'd given up. It was for finally finding what he'd been looking for. Probably all day.

Elaina shook her head as he approached, but Maggie could hear her labored breathing. Both she and Jordan backed up against the window as Duncan wrapped his arms around Elaina's waist and kissed her without uttering a word. For a moment Elaina remained rigid, unmoving, but Maggie watched as she relaxed into the kiss, and she and Jordan let out a collective sigh.

"Ladies," Duncan said when he finally came up for air, bowing his head in greeting. "M-My apologies for being late." His voice shook, and he stammered on his words, yet still he exuded that charm she remembered. There were a lot of things Maggie forgot, but you didn't forget someone like Duncan McAllister. Despite whatever he'd been through today—and whatever hell Elaina was about to drag him through—Maggie couldn't help but smile in his presence.

He kissed Jordan on the cheek. "Congratulations on the engagement," he said, and Jordan gasped. Maggie received a kiss as well. "I bet you're right proud of Griffin getting that job in Washington. I'd love to stay and chat, but I have a wedding to save."

He turned back to Elaina, and Maggie could see the temporary spell of the kiss evaporate as Elaina's eyes narrowed at her fiancé. Duncan opened his mouth to say something to her, but she stormed out the back door and onto the beach. Still carrying his messenger bag slung across his body, he didn't hesitate before chasing after her, leaving Maggie and Jordan stunned in his wake.

Noah and Griffin made their way through the confused crowd until they stood in front of what looked like a delightedly silent Jordan and a horrified Maggie.

Here she thought she was being ridiculous, worrying when there was nothing she could place her finger on to worry about. Turns out she didn't need to wait for the *other* shoe to drop. They were both dropping at the same damned time.

"What?" Noah asked. Jordan's eyes were brimming with tears.

"Why…" Jordan hiccupped again, and Maggie remembered the ouzo. Maybe she misunderstood what Duncan said. Maybe it was just her low tolerance for liquor. "Why…" Jordan continued, "did Duncan just congratulate me on my engagement?"

"Jesus, Duncan," Noah said, running a hand through his hair. "This wasn't how this was supposed to happen."

"Shit," Griffin mumbled under his breath. His eyes locked on Maggie's, and she knew he wanted to say something, to answer the dread he must have seen in her eyes, but neither of them would interrupt Noah and Jordan's unexpected moment.

"Brooks," Noah said, his voice soft and low, but it didn't matter. The room went silent as he dropped to one knee and fumbled in his bag until he produced a small velvet box.

Jordan hiccupped again, but this time it wasn't the alcohol. It was a small sob, and Maggie's gut twisted. Jordan and Noah's lives were changing right in front of her, in the best possible way. And after she said yes—because of course she would—Griffin was going to confirm what Duncan spoiled for her, that Griffin was moving to Washington and leaving her behind. What the hell was in Washington? Did Duncan mean D.C.? God, was he taking a job somehow connected to his father's political aspirations? How much did she not know about the man she lived with?

Maggie's head swam again. Stupid ouzo. Stupid Maggie for thinking she was safe from being knocked on her ass by anything life threw at her anymore. She may have been standing in everyone else's eyes, but inside she was grasping for purchase, doing everything she could to stay upright.

Jordan covered her mouth with her hands as tears streamed down her face, and all Maggie wished was that this moment and what she knew would come after could be fast-forwarded, just so she was sure she made it through. Instead, time seemed to slow down. Griffin grabbed her hand, tried to thread his fingers through hers, but she pulled away, his touch too much to bear.

Noah opened the box before speaking again, revealing a round solitaire diamond ring. It might not have been huge, but Maggie's front-row seat confirmed it was beautiful.

"God," he started. "I wasn't supposed to do this off the cuff, you know? I had the right moment in my head. Everything was going to be perfect." He chuckled. "But perfect has never been our way, has it?"

Jordan shook her head, still cupping her hands to her mouth.

"I fell for you as soon as I met you, Brooks. Being stuck with you in a train vestibule should have put me into a freaking panic attack, but instead it made me realize what I didn't even know I was missing."

Jordan let her hands fall, one of them reaching for Noah's cheek. He leaned into her palm and kissed it.

"I got a lot wrong that year," he continued. "But the one thing I got right was not letting you get away. Thank you for not giving up on me." He dropped her hand so he could remove the ring from the box. "I love you, Brooks. It doesn't matter that it's been three years. Every day I wake up with you next to me is like falling for you all over again. I know our lives are crazy right now, but I also know we'll get through it. Because we're *us*." He cleared his throat and held the ring up to her. "Let's be us always, Brooks. Marry me."

Jordan nodded as he slid the ring onto her finger. Then he rose to meet her.

"Say the word, Brooks." Noah glanced around at their captive audience. "Everyone's waiting for you to say it out loud. I'd kind of like to hear it, too."

Jordan let out a laughing sob and then cupped his cheeks in her hands. "Yes, I'll marry you, Noah. I love you. I want to be us. Always."

The room erupted in applause as the newly engaged couple kissed, no one the wiser that outside, tomorrow's groom was most likely trying to convince the bride to still have him, or that right in the very room where a couple just promised their lives to each other, another was on the brink of falling apart.

"We need to talk."

Griffin's hand was around Maggie's wrist, and he was pulling her back toward the door and out into the main restaurant.

But it didn't really matter what he was about to say, because after a year of trusting the first person outside of her gran and Miles, Griffin had lied to her. She was always so afraid that letting him into her life was a risk for *him*—that somehow he'd end up getting hurt. But she'd had it all wrong. Because here they were, thousands of miles from home, on what should have been the best weekend they'd ever had, and the only thing she was sure of now was that whatever Griffin said next would break *her* heart.

Chapter Seventeen

DUNCAN

Duncan was really tired of running, so it was a good thing the sand was there to slow Elaina down. He caught up to her quickly, grabbing her hand and forcing her to face him.

The sun hadn't quite set yet, the glare of the waning light bouncing off the waves and backlighting the woman in front of him. Even with the hindrance of his swollen eye, he marveled at how Elaina still took his breath away. From the second he'd seen her, he knew that it wasn't marrying her that had tripped him up this morning. He had no doubt that she was the only person he could fathom giving his life to. But the big picture? Leaving his home for the unknown? Well, that was fucking terrifying, and Elaina should understand at least that—the reason why he took his eyes off his damn bag and let this day turn to complete and utter shite.

"Are you going to say something, or are you just going to stare at me like a pirate?"

Duncan couldn't help it. He threw back his head and

laughed—a full-on howl. His eyes even watered a bit—well, the good one did, at least. He realized he hadn't really let go of the stress of the day, and no matter how angry Elaina was at him, being in her presence washed away all the rest.

Elaina took advantage of his moment of weakness and stalked off toward the water again. The wind whipped at them wildly, and he watched as she cupped her shoulders in her hands, rubbing them to keep warm.

"I could warm you up," he said as he approached, and Elaina whirled on him, arms crossed.

"You don't call me the whole day. Just a text that says, *Forgive me. I couldn't get on the second plane.* What am I supposed to think? You make me lie to my family...*and* yours. You come here looking like—like—I don't even know *what* you look like. But you do not look like the man I'm supposed to marry in the morning."

He staggered back, this time not because she took his breath away but because she knocked the wind out of him.

"My phone was dead. And that arsehole security bloke only let me make one call on his phone." He ran a hand through his hair. "That doesn't even matter. Wha' am I supposed to look like, Elaina? If I showed up at ten o'clock this morning, hair combed and face free of any sign that would remind you of what you really see when you look at me, would you forget that I'm a mess sometimes? That I make mistakes? That I'm not a perfect man? I never pretended to be anything other than what I was. But you never really accepted that. Did ya, now?"

Elaina huffed out a breath but squeezed her arms tighter.

Three years ago, he had loved that she was a challenge—someone to whom he had to prove himself worthy. But had he ever really proved anything? Or had she just let her heart overrule her head until now? He knew he was a good man, that he loved her, and all this time he thought that was enough.

Was he always on time? No. Did he still like to have, on occasion, one more pint than his body's self-imposed limit? Of course. He wasn't going to apologize for that, except on the rare occasion when he woke up on the Haudagain Roundabout back home in Aberdeen, but that hadn't happened in two years. And then it was only two other times before that. Christ, he liked to have fun, but he knew how to be a responsible adult when the time called for it. But did Elaina have that faith in him?

"I think you wanted to get angry with me today. And fucking hell—I gave you good reason." Duncan paced now. He was so ready to beg for her forgiveness that he hadn't realized he was bloody angry, too. "You want to know why I didn't call you, Elaina? Why I chose Griffin over you?"

Elaina flinched at his words, and something twisted in his gut, but it was like he was a runaway train—full-steam ahead, no matter what came out of his mouth.

"Because I knew he wouldn't judge me. He lives on another continent. I haven't seen him in more than a year. But I knew if I called him, he'd show up—no questions asked. And hell, Elaina. That's what he did. What if it was you on the other end of that call? What if I had called you?"

Even in the fading light, he could see her skin pricked with goose bumps. He ached to press his palms to her shoulders and rub her flesh warm. But it was like the beach was made of quicksand, rooting them in their anger and stubbornness.

At first she said nothing, so he waited. What was the rush? It wasn't as if there was a restaurant full of people waiting for them.

Finally, Elaina let out a long sigh, which to Duncan was admission enough. But still, he waited.

"I do not know," she admitted.

But he did. Duncan knew he loved this woman, but he also knew she would have chosen anger over understanding.

He knew from her narrowed eyes as soon as he saw her that she had already judged him.

"I don' know where tha' leaves us," he said. Then he opened his bag, the one he risked missing his own wedding to save, and pulled out the tartan scarf. She didn't flinch when he took a step toward her, close enough for him to drape the fabric over the pebbled skin of her shoulders.

"*This* is why I was late," he said, letting his hands linger on top of the scarf—on *her.* "It's why I look the way I do. I let the bag out of my sight for one bloody second, and it was stolen. I chased the arsehole. I did. But I guess you can see that didn't turn out like I'd planned." He patted the messenger bag slung across his body. When he stepped back, she grabbed the tartan edges tight. Elaina's eyes shone with not-yet-fallen tears, and something caught in Duncan's throat. It wasn't a sob, because if there was one thing Duncan McAllister did not do, it was cry. On a beach. In what felt like some sort of tragic scene in a romantic movie.

He swallowed hard, unsure what this moment was or what it meant for them. All he knew was that this didn't feel much like a celebration.

"I look like shite," he said. "You're right about that. But I feel like shite, too. I'm going in there and saying hello to my mum and dad—to yours, too. I'm going to have some food, maybe a pint or two, and then I'm going to the hotel. I think we need to decide what's happening tomorrow, Elaina. I think we need to—"

"Duncan," she said, her voice cracking on the first syllable. But he shook his head.

"I don't want you to have to pretend with me," he said. "I don't want you to expect me to mess up and then judge me when I do. And I definitely don't want you to wish I was anyone other than who I am. Because I never wished that about you."

He held out his hand, and she looked down at it, then back up at him.

"Let's walk in together, aye? No matter what happens now, I love you. And I know it's not been an easy day. So we'll eat—and drink—and when you're ready, we'll talk."

Elaina laced her fingers through his, her skin cold against his warmth.

Duncan waited for some other response. What? He didn't know.

Elaina Tripoli collected herself. She didn't cry. She no longer seemed like she wanted to yell. And she followed him inside.

Chapter Eighteen

G riffin sat at an empty two-top in a far corner of the unused restaurant. Maggie didn't follow his lead.

"Please sit?" he said, but it came out like a question.

Freaking Duncan. Maybe they should have skipped the champagne on the short flight. Maybe when a guy was having one of the shittiest days of his life, it wasn't the time to unload personal secrets on him. *Maybe* he never should have kept a secret from Maggie in the first place. But here they were, him sitting, pleading—and her barely able to look at him.

"Pippi. *Please.*"

She sat, and she even let her eyes meet his, but those emerald eyes that always grounded him, that let him know how much he was loved, were distant. Unrecognizable.

"I'm sitting," she said. "But you don't get to call me that, Griffin. Not now."

He nodded. "Fair enough." He had a captive audience, and at least that was a start. "Can I ask…what did Duncan tell you?"

Maggie scoffed out a bitter laugh, something so unlike her, and it felt like a needle pricking his skin. He'd brought this out in her, and he hated himself for it.

"Do you need to check to make sure your story matches up with his?" she asked.

He shook his head. He was going about this all wrong. But didn't she know him enough to understand that when it came to her, his intentions were always good? Everything came from a place of loving her, a place he didn't know was capable of existing inside him until she entered his life.

"That's not what I meant," he said. "Maggie…I didn't lie to you. I didn't mean to, anyway."

She just sat there, a statue, eyes on him, yet some sort of invisible barrier kept her from seeing him.

He reached into the pocket of his jeans. *God, look at her in that dress.* He was travel weary, and he knew he needed a shower. He felt out of place in her clean elegance. Her undeniable beauty—and her never-wavering honesty.

"Here," he said, sliding the folded piece of paper across the table. "I was just waiting for the right time to tell you."

She unfolded the congratulatory letter, her movements slow and deliberate. And then she read.

Upon reading the first line, Maggie gasped, her hand flying to her mouth. She couldn't hold back the involuntary smile, but she shuttered the expression as quickly as it came. Even when she was angry at him, when she felt the sting of betrayal, she was happy for him. But delaying the truth had robbed her of sharing in his joy.

When she finished reading, she refolded the letter and slid it back across the table to him. It took her a few moments to look up, and when she did, she wore a smile—one that didn't reach her eyes and didn't make that spot on top of her nose crinkle the way he loved.

"I'm proud of you," she said. "I was afraid when Duncan said Washington that you'd gone back to your father. But this? This is really good. I'm sure you'll be really happy in D.C."

Her fingers were still on the paper, and she fidgeted with it in the silence.

He laid a hand on hers to stop her nervous motion.

"I didn't accept it, Maggie. Not yet. I wouldn't—not without you."

Her smile morphed into one he knew was real, but it was also sad.

She bit her lip. "But you applied for it without me."

He had, and at the time it didn't seem like a big deal.

"I didn't think I'd get it," he said. "It was just a *what if?* It wasn't anything we needed to talk about because it wasn't going to happen."

She pulled her hand away and crossed her arms over her chest, squeezing herself tight. Griffin wanted those to be *his* arms around her. And they would be soon, right? He hadn't done something irrevocable. Had he?

"It *did* happen," she said. "When did the letter come?"

"When you came home sick."

Maggie's eyes widened, and she pushed back her chair and stood from the table.

"And *you* didn't think I could handle it?"

He rose to meet her and placed his hands on her cheeks.

"It wasn't the right time to talk about something this big. You were… And then we…"

The words weren't coming out right, so he pulled out the big guns and tried to kiss her. If they could just reconnect, she'd understand. But Maggie's hands were on his wrists like lightning, forcing him to drop his hands to his sides.

"I get it," she said. "I was too much of a mess then to tell me. And then all those hours we spent on the plane together when I felt perfectly fine, you just assumed I'd fall apart? That

I couldn't handle the news? That I was weak?" Maggie took a step back, her hard stare rooting him in place. "It's not just the letter, Griffin. You didn't even tell me you were applying for this fellowship in the first place." She paused for a long breath. "You convinced me that you believed in me," she said.

"I do!" he blurted out. "Jesus, Maggie. I have always believed in you. I *still* believe in you." His voice was frantic. Irrevocable was starting to feel like a real possibility, and he was clawing, tooth and nail, to make her hear.

She shook her head, and he knew he was losing his grip. They were on a ledge, and she was about to fall off. Or worse—she was going to knock him off and watch him fall.

"There are only two explanations for you keeping this from me. The first is because you still see me as I saw myself for two years—weak. The second…is that this had nothing to do with me in the first place, that you're leaving and waiting for the right time to tell me."

Griffin dropped both hands to the table and bent forward, trying to catch his breath. He wanted to argue with her on both counts. The truth was, he didn't see her as weak. That was never the case. But he had placed her in his own glass cabinet—beautiful and fragile, only to be taken out with the utmost care. He hadn't meant to, but he'd just proven to her that's what he'd done.

And what about the second part?

"You're right," he said, straightening to face her, and her breathing hitched at his words. "Not the way you think you are, though. You're the strongest person I know, Maggie. You might not believe me, but that doesn't mean I'm lying." He ran a hand through his hair. "No matter how twisted their means, the only way my parents know how to love me is to protect me from fucking up. My sisters, too. People have always picked up the pieces for me until I finally had the balls to step out on my own. But I guess the apple doesn't fall too far, huh? Guess

I can't escape being a Reed when it's all I know."

He let out a bitter laugh. Maggie was the catalyst for him to change his life. After always taking the easy way out, Griffin cut himself off from his family's financial support, choosing a job that paid next to nothing but made him happy instead of working for his father. All he'd ever wanted to do was break free from the hold his family had on him and be his own person. But he still couldn't escape being just like them, treating Maggie how they'd always treated him.

"I thought by waiting I was protecting you—"

"I don't need protecting," she interrupted.

He nodded. "I know." Then he let out a long sigh. "But I was protecting me, too."

"From what?"

He knew she was still mad, but that didn't stop him. He grabbed her hand and squeezed, bringing her knuckles to his lips. He just needed at least one part of her close, to maintain the connection before it was lost for good.

"From wanting two things I might not be able to have."

"You *have* to take this fellowship," she said. "You can't turn down something like this."

He kept his lips pressed to her skin as he spoke. "I can't go without you," he said. "I can't chase this dream if you don't chase it with me."

Maggie inhaled, and he heard the shaking in her breath. Not a good sign. He closed his eyes as he waited for her to respond.

"It's not my dream," she said. "And I love you, more than you can imagine, but I can't let you be my only dream. And I can't let you jeopardize yours by thinking you need to protect me."

He opened his mouth to argue, but she cut him off.

"You just admitted it yourself. The only thing that's changed in my daily life is adding more classes, and you're already afraid I'm going to break. What will happen if I uproot my life and go with you? How will you be able to focus on you if you're always worrying about me?"

He pulled her to him now, and she didn't protest. Griffin pressed his lips to her forehead, then her eyes and cheeks. Finally her lips. She kissed him back.

"It's only a year," she said, but there was nothing convincing in her tone. Griffin had always found something special about kissing away her tears, tasting the salt on his tongue along with everything Maggie. Yet somehow he knew it that night he opened the letter just as he did now—these tears meant the end of *something*. Maybe not the end of them, not yet. Though as close as he held her…and as much as she clung to him as well…the distance began to grow, and would eventually put hundreds of miles between them.

"Yeah," he whispered, sure that he would lose it if he tried to speak out loud. "It's only a year."

Chapter Nineteen

MILES

"What is this?" Miles asked, sipping his beer. His fingertips brushed the edge of a picture frame, but instead of a photograph, inside it sat an acceptance letter to the University of Virginia.

Alex was popping the top off his own bottle. He shrugged as he made his way to the small space that doubled as a kitchen eating area and small living space.

"I'm going to guess that you can read," he said to Miles, a tightness to his voice he seemed to want to disguise with his disarming smile.

So Miles decided to prove Alex's assumption. He read aloud.

"Dear Mr. Karas... We are delighted to welcome you to the University of Virginia's College of Liberal Arts and Sciences as well as the Cavaliers' men's soccer team—"

Alex tipped the frame over softly so it laid facedown on the shelf where it sat.

"Just proving you right," Miles said. "Been reading since I was three. I'm precocious like that. Do you find my precociousness adorable?" he teased, and Alex ignored him, brushing past his shoulder and collapsing onto a small couch.

"So you went to the University of Virginia?" Miles asked.

Alex shook his head, then let out a long breath.

"I went to the City University of New York and then came back to Greece for culinary training, the only thing my father would pay for."

Miles sat down next to him. He hadn't wanted to know Alex's name a few hours ago, and now here he was in the man's apartment, on the brink of learning his history. His first instinct was to kiss him, to keep the past at bay even if it was only Alex's and not his own. But when Alex turned to face him, their knees bumping as he did, Miles could tell Alex wanted, maybe needed, to tell him the rest of the story, so he let him.

"What happened with Virginia?" Miles asked.

Alex took a swig of his beer.

"I broke my leg the spring before my first year, playing on my secondary school's team."

Miles laid a hand on Alex's knee, the gesture so natural he hadn't realized he'd done it until Alex let his own hand rest on top of it.

"They took away your scholarship for an injury?" Miles asked, still not understanding.

Alex shook his head. "They took away my scholarship because I had to have three surgeries to fix my leg, because I'm lucky I can even walk on my own. Playing again was never an option, which meant the University of Virginia wasn't an option anymore, either."

Miles's heart twisted at the thought of losing something like that.

"I'm sorry," he said. "Shit, I'm really sorry."

Alex took another swig from his bottle.

"I'm not," he said. "Don't get me wrong. I spent a long time wallowing. I couldn't even attend university the first year I was supposed to because of the surgeries and missing deadlines for applying anywhere for that fall semester. So yeah, I wallowed for a good few years until I found cooking. And then life just sort of clicked."

He squeezed Miles's hand over his knee, and Miles felt something shift in the air between them.

"Wait," he said. "If you're not sorry that it happened, why did it bother you when I started reading the letter?"

Alex drained the last of his bottle and then set it on the table next to the frame, which he promptly righted.

"I love that letter," he said. "It's a reminder that losing something doesn't mean losing *everything*, but I haven't heard the words on that page in a long time. Hearing it in your voice? I don't know, it was the past and the present colliding like it hasn't before."

Alex shifted so he sat straight instead of reclined against the cushions. Both hands now free, he brought a hand to Miles's neck, urging him closer. Miles didn't resist, bowing his head toward Alex, who stopped him before their lips could touch.

"I showed you mine," he said. "You show me yours."

"What?" Miles asked. "What do you want from me?"

"I want more than your name," Alex admitted. "I want some little piece to attach to the memory of what you taste like." He flicked his tongue against Miles's bottom lip.

"Why?" Miles didn't like where this was going.

"Why not?" Alex asked. "No expectations," he added. "Just give me a sense of who you are."

Miles squeezed his eyes shut. Because there was an expectation. Alex had invited him to stay for the weekend, but what did Miles think? That the guy would be satisfied with nothing but a name for three days? Still, he hadn't signed up for this. The more he gave to Alex, the less safe he would be.

"I'm the guy who's shit when it comes to sharing," he said, and Alex brushed his lips with a small kiss.

"Were you always?" he asked, and Miles couldn't help it. He shook his head. He *wanted* Alex to know at least this.

"Well then," Alex said, kissing him again. "That's a start."

Miles lay on his back, hand behind his head. He figured he should probably text Maggie and make sure she was doing okay without him. Hell, he didn't even know if Griffin had made it back yet, but he wasn't sure where exactly his jeans were. Or his shirt. His boxer briefs were probably nearest, since they'd been the last to come off, but he couldn't really be sure. One thing was certain—he wouldn't have access to his phone until he went on a naked scavenger hunt for his clothes.

But Alex stood in the open doorway of the bedroom now, the tray he held across his midsection the only thing giving him any sort of coverage at all. Not that Miles wanted any part of the man in front of him blocked from view.

Shit. This man was a sight, bare and beautiful and ready to sate him in a wholly different way than he just had. It had been hard enough for the two of them to make it from the living area to the bedroom, mostly because Miles had been— well—*hard.* Every time Alex's lips touched his, Miles's body ached for more. And once they finished what they started on the plane, he knew he'd say yes to anything this man asked of him this weekend. Maybe he didn't commit long-term, but he sure as hell had pledged his entire being to Alex for the seventy-two hours he'd be in Greece.

"You look hungry," Alex said, and Miles caught himself

licking his lips. He was starving, the last full meal he ate in Minneapolis seeming like it was days ago.

Alex set the tray on the side table next to the bed and crawled back in next to Miles.

They fit together like instinct, as if there was no question that when Alex slipped under the sheet, Miles would drape a leg over his and pull him into another kiss. Because hungry as he was for whatever was on that tray, he craved the taste of Alex on his lips just that much more.

"You are delicious," he said, and Alex let out a small moan mixed with a deep, sexy laugh.

"*You* need to eat," he told Miles, sliding away just enough so that Miles and his ready-to-go-again erection were no longer pressing against Alex's thigh. "Let me feed you," Alex continued, reaching over to the tray and coming back with something that looked like a green egg roll. "And then"—he teased Miles's parted lips with his tongue—"I'll *feed* you."

Miles growled under his breath. This weekend would be the end of him for sure, but what a fucking way to go.

He propped himself up on one elbow and raised a brow at the item between Alex's fingers.

"*Dolmathes*," Alex said, answering his unspoken question.

Miles narrowed his eyes. "Does not compute."

Alex laughed. "Grape leaves stuffed with rice, pine nuts, onion, dill…they're my specialty, so you'd better think they are exquisite or else lie and say they are anyway."

Alex held a napkin under Miles's chin, kissed him, and then lifted the green egg roll to his lips. Miles opened his mouth and bit down, olive oil dribbling from his chin and onto the napkin. He may not have been a foodie, but he knew enough to understand that he would never eat a *dolmathe* prepared by anyone else ever again.

"Jesus," Miles said after swallowing. He licked the tangy oil from his lips. *Was that lemon juice mixed in there?*

Alex popped the second half in his own mouth. "Most people call me Alex."

Miles rolled his eyes. Alex made a move to clean his hand on the napkin, but Miles grabbed his wrist before he could do it, licking the tips of his finger and thumb.

Alex closed his eyes and sighed. Miles knew the napkin would do a better job, but he couldn't let an opportunity to savor the taste of his skin go to waste. In fact, as absolutely exquisite as the *dolmathe* was, he had an appetite for something else entirely.

He climbed over Alex, straddling him, Miles's hard length pressed against Alex's hip.

"Are you sure you don't have to help out at the party?" he asked, and Alex shook his head.

"That was the deal, since I was only arriving back from New York this morning—finish food preparations for this evening and tomorrow, and I get the night off. The serving staff is taking care of the rest."

Miles wrapped both of his hands around Alex's wrists, pinning his arms above his head as he sampled what he craved, starting with full, inviting lips.

"In that case," Miles said when he took a breath, "I'd like to satisfy my appetite, if you don't mind."

He held Alex's wrists above his head as he kissed his stubbled jaw and neck.

"I don't mind," Alex told him, his voice low and hoarse.

When Miles needed the use of his hands to support his own body weight, he repositioned Alex's on the low headboard.

"Don't let go," he said, just the hint of command in his voice.

Alex gave him an amused grin, but his eyes were hungry with need.

"Yes, sir," he said, and Miles continued his descent down

the length of this beautiful man's body, kissing and sucking until he found the trail of fine dark hair, the map to his desired destination. Only when he dipped under the sheet, his expression safe from detection, did he let his overconfident grin fade.

Man or woman, Miles had never had a preference. He found both beautiful in their own ways and understood that his sexual connection came from a place deeper than the physical, which was why he was both terrified and insatiable. He couldn't get enough of the man who lay beneath him. It had been so long since he'd wanted someone as much as he wanted Alex, and here he was, ripe for the taking and his—*all* his—for two more days. And then what? Alex said he wanted more than just his name, but it was only to remember him. That's what he'd said. Not to deepen their bond past the physical. Miles enjoyed the hell out of the physical, but what did it mean that Alex fed him in bed, made him laugh, and made him somehow feel safe when he was thousands of miles from home?

He didn't want to think. Instead he swirled his tongue around Alex's tip, the tang of salt on his taste buds. Then Miles took his solid length into his mouth and lost himself in desire.

Two more days, he thought as Alex writhed beneath him. *Two more days and then good-bye*—because what was the alternative?

There wasn't one, not a single scenario where Miles could test the waters—see how far his appetite could take him or if he'd ever admit to himself what couldn't possibly be true after only one day: that Miles was hungry for more than food or the sweet agony of what Alex did to him physically.

The thing he'd so easily avoided when he called the shots flew out the window when a seven-hour flight took away what he'd maintained for years—control. And now that thing, that need, was creeping up from the depths and threatening to tear down his carefully constructed fortress.

Connection. Miles hadn't known he'd wanted it, needed it, had been *missing* it until he got a taste of the possibility.

What if there was no flight on Sunday evening?

What if Alex wasn't threatened by his sexuality?

What if something more didn't have to mean something he would lose?

Alex came on a shudder under Miles's expert care, yet none of it really mattered, did it? Because there *was* a flight. Once Alex knew Miles was bi, things would change. And wanting what he couldn't keep always ended in loss.

Chapter Twenty

DUNCAN

Duncan played the part of the fiancé who was grateful to make it back to his almost-wife. He had tables of inebriated Greeks and Scots in tears of laughter as he recounted the day's ordeal, making light of what might possibly have been the turning point in his relationship with Elaina.

This was how Elaina learned the whole story—not directly from him but second-hand as he entertained their guests, Duncan's father slapping him on the back in congratulations for taking a fist to the face in the name of love; Elaina's mother kissing him on both cheeks and thanking him repeatedly in Greek, *Efharistó. Efharistó*, for the special token he'd brought for her daughter. Add to that the excitement of Jordan and Noah's engagement that maybe wasn't supposed to happen just then, and no one seemed to notice the growing tension between him and his wife-to-be, that they hadn't touched or kissed other than when family members demanded a preview of that moment after they both said, "I do."

But the show was over now. Elaina's family was strict on tradition, so despite the many, *many* nights he and Elaina had spent in the same bed while they lived in Scotland, going home together the night before the wedding was severely off-limits. So Duncan lay in his hotel bed alone with a melting bag of ice on his face and the balcony door ajar so he could listen to the rhythmic beat of the waves lapping at the shore. He had hoped the cadence would lull him to sleep, but his brain refused to cooperate, so all he could do was analyze his reunion with Elaina and what it meant for the events that were supposed to follow in the morning.

He looked at his phone. One in the morning. *Shite.* He'd been laying there an hour already and felt no more sure about what was supposed to happen next than he had when he'd walked into the room. Alone.

Of course, this was how it was supposed to go—Duncan in the hotel and Elaina in her parents' apartment. Tomorrow they were to spend their first night as husband and wife together in a suite that would be decorated by Elaina's family prior to their arrival. Now he wasn't so sure.

A soft knock sounded, and for a second he couldn't tell if it came from his door or the one next to his room. He waited, and the sound came again, still light but louder than before, so he rose to see who it was. With his good eye to the peephole, he could see the back of Elaina's head, but he was certain it was her. He gripped the door handle and pressed down, the audible *click* deafening in the tense silence. He'd only gotten the door open a crack when he felt resistance.

"Put the chain on so it will only open enough for you to hear me," she said, and Duncan could hear that she'd been crying. His throat tightened, and his instinct was to throw the door open and pull her to him, to promise her that everything would be fine even when he knew that might be a lie. But he also knew her superstitions about the wedding day, and technically it was the day of the wedding. He wasn't supposed to *see* her until the ceremony.

So he did as she asked, chaining the top of the door and pulling it open only as far as the chain would allow. Then he slid down the wall next to the small opening. Elaina did the same, keeping her back to him. He wanted to argue that she was bending the rules, that technically he *could* see her, but he refrained, not wanting to do anything that might send her away.

"You could have phoned," he said. "Would have been easier, aye?"

She shook her head, her black waves tumbling over her shoulders. Elaina no longer wore the dress that had left him breathless but instead sat before him in an oversize cable-knit jumper and jeans. He recognized that jumper and realized it was the one that started the snowball effect of the day's events. He'd removed it again at the party, lain it over a chair, and forgotten about it. Now here was his fiancée, face most likely tear-stained, and her body enveloped in *his* clothes. Earlier today he had hated that jumper. It was to blame, after all.

But now he wanted to bury his face in the itchy wool, breathe in his scent mixed with hers, and— *Fuck*. What were they doing?

"I don't want this to be easy," she said, and something in his heart lurched. What was *this*?

"Wha' are we doin' here, Elaina? Why'd you come?"

She cleared her throat, and he could feel that she was gearing up for something big.

"I was wrong," she started, and he held his breath, not only for Elaina uttering words he'd never heard her say but because he wasn't sure he could take whatever she said next. "I was wrong to say yes to marrying you when as much as I loved you, I hadn't fully accepted you. Not the way I should have."

Duncan had to tell himself to exhale. Then to inhale again. Breathing was no longer involuntary, and depending on what Elaina said next, he might not remember to take that next breath.

"You were right," she continued. "I judged you and had expectations that were not based on who you are but on who I thought my future husband should be."

He heard a hitch in her breath and watched Elaina's shoulders rise and fall. If anything was clear to him tonight, it was that Elaina may have loved him, but she loved a version of him that didn't exist yet and may not ever.

"I am sorry," she said, her voice small and like nothing he'd ever heard before.

Elaina Tripoli was a force to be reckoned with, and Duncan wasn't sure how to reconcile the woman he knew with the one sitting before him now. It looked like they both still had a lot to learn about each other.

"I love you, Duncan. But you deserve better than what I gave you today. You deserve someone who would never doubt you and who would never expect you to be anyone other than who you are. I know you might not believe me, but I fell in love with the boy you were when I met you."

He reached a hand through the crack in the door, the tips of his fingers just barely making contact with hers. She didn't flinch, and he told himself that if he maintained contact—an almost-touch—that this evening wouldn't be the end they were barreling toward.

"Elaina," he said, his strained voice unrecognizable to his own ears.

"Let me finish," she said, and he waited. "I fell in love with the boy you were because I knew you'd become the man you were meant to be. And you *have*, Duncan. I should have seen that. I should have *trusted* that. But instead I conjured up unrealistic expectations of what I believed was perfection, and because of that I was not the woman I should have been for you. I see that now."

She let out a long, shuddering breath, and he remained quiet. He did not move his hand, though, his fingertips still pressed to hers.

"I cannot promise you that I will change my way of thinking overnight, but I will try. For *you* I will try to be the woman you deserve. I will be at the church in the morning. If you come, I will marry you. If you do not—if I have put the final straw on top of the camel—I will understand."

Duncan's lips teased at a smile, if only for a second. He could spend the rest of his life listening to Elaina's rephrasing of English idioms. He wanted to teach her some of his family's sayings, like the one his great-gran always said when Duncan's father would get on him about his marks in school: *Failing means you're playing.*

In other words, it was better to be shite at something than not to be taking part in it at all.

For fuck's sake. That was it. Maybe they'd mucked things up right and left today—and plenty of other times in the past three years—but he and Elaina were active participants in this relationship. They weren't just sitting by waiting for things to happen. He sprang to his feet to unlatch the chain, not having realized what he should have already known when the tips of his fingers went cold.

Elaina was gone.

He scrambled to his bedside table and unlocked his phone, his fingers furious against the uncooperative keys and the equally arse-like autocorrect. It took him three tries just to get out, *You didn't let me finish.* He waited the requisite amount of time for her to make it back to her home above Ambrosia. Then he waited several minutes more—and several more after that.

But there was no response.

Who did Elaina Tripoli think she was, coming to his room and being all grandiose and selfless? Apologizing, even, for the love of ouzo…and Duncan did love the stuff. Fucking hell, who was this woman promising to try to be better and then walking away before he could catch his breath—before he could tell her the answer to his own question.

She was the reason he could only see out of one eye at the moment.

She was the woman who drove him mad with his anticipation of her reaction to his…detainment in Athens.

She was the woman who scared him the most, but wasn't Duncan McAllister the kind of guy who enjoyed a little bit of risk?

Elaina Tripoli was the woman he loved, even when they made a right mess of things.

She was his fiancée, and in a few short hours, he would don his kilt and make her his wife.

Chapter Twenty-One

NOAH

Noah sat at the foot of the bed, head in his hands. He got up and paced the length of the room a few times. Then it was back to the bed.

She had said *yes.* Jordan had said *yes.* Of course she had. She loved him. Or maybe it was more… *Of course she did. She had an audience.* Jesus, what if that was why she'd agreed?

He flopped down on the bed, flat on his back, and closed his eyes. On any other day he would have joined Jordan in the shower, especially since tonight's was purely gratuitous, her need to experience "the best water pressure ever" for the second time that day. But right now he couldn't shake the feeling that something was off.

She'd cried. She'd said yes. She'd let him put the ring on her finger. Everything happened as he'd wanted it to happen. Except for one thing.

It wasn't *where* it was supposed to happen. Or when. Okay, so maybe that was two things. But he realized those two things were it. This proposal was supposed to undo the crap they went through in Aberdeen and turn all of Jordan's memories of that place into new and improved ones. He didn't want her to remember the year they met in Scotland as one where he'd pushed her away, scared that what they'd felt wouldn't survive once they were back in the real world, separated by geography. He didn't begrudge her the happy times she had without him. She'd deserved that. And they did get it right in the end, even making the long-distance thing work until Jordan had moved to Columbus for grad school. But that didn't change that they had wasted those months in Aberdeen. Every time he thought about what it would have been like to spend that time abroad together instead of apart, he kind of wanted to punch himself in the throat.

He took in a deep breath, ignoring the tiny shudder as he exhaled.

"Hey."

Noah's eyes widened at the sound of Jordan's voice. He hadn't realized the shower had stopped.

"Hey," he said, eyes trained on the blades of the ceiling fan above him.

Jordan perched on the side of the bed, wearing nothing but the hotel robe.

"You gonna make some room for me?"

He rotated his head from side to side, taking note of his arms sprawled out from his shoulders. He motioned for her to come closer.

"There's *always* room for you, Brooks."

She smiled, the simplest of gestures yet one that made him melt just a little every time she did it. Then she burrowed into the space between his arm and his body, her wet hair soaking through his T-shirt, but he didn't care. He pulled her closer, prepared for the entirety of his garment to act as her towel, so long as she stayed connected to him like this.

"I kinda thought you'd join me," she said, a small pout on her lips.

"Oh, right," he started. "Lost in thought, I guess."

She kissed his chest.

"It's okay. I get it. You had a long day. I just missed you," she said. "But that was a really cool thing you did, you and Griffin."

He kissed the top of her head.

"I missed you, too. And by cool thing, do you mean rescuing Duncan from airport prison or making the wise choice to show him the engagement ring so he could ruin my proposal?"

Jordan pushed herself up on her elbow. This time Noah wasn't melting because she sure as hell wasn't smiling.

"What?" he asked.

First her eyes narrowed, then widened. He couldn't tell if she was angry or confused. Or maybe sad? What was that look? He thought he knew all her expressions, but apparently he'd never elicited this one before.

"*Ruined your proposal?* Did you—did you *not* want to propose to me?"

He sprang up, nearly launching her off the edge of the bed.

"No! I wasn't going to… I mean, yes! Jordan…I'm sorry. Shit. That's not what I meant. I just—it wasn't supposed to happen. Not *yet*. Not *here*. I bought a ring," he insisted. "You know I want to marry you."

"And I want to marry you, too." She sighed. "But don't you get it? I have pictured this day—this moment—in my head a thousand times. No matter what the scenario, it always ended in me saying *yes*. But never once did I envision *you* regretting any part of it."

A sharp knock sounded on the door, and they both startled. Jordan rolled off the bed and strode to answer it.

"Robe," Noah called. "You're only wearing a robe, Brooks."

But she didn't comment. Instead she threw open the door to find Griffin standing, poised to knock again.

"Shit," Griffin said, catching himself before knocking on Jordan's forehead. "Sorry."

"What's going on?" she asked, and he shrugged.

"Maggie and I kind of— We're in the middle of— I know this is shitty to ask after you two just got engaged and everything, but I need a place to…"

He stopped mid–awkward sentence, his eyes volleying from Jordan to Noah and back to Jordan again.

"You guys don't look like I imagine happily engaged is supposed to look."

"I'm going to change," Jordan said, and she grabbed clothes out of her suitcase and slipped back into the bathroom.

"Are you going somewhere?" Griffin asked her, and she glanced at Noah.

Noah sighed.

"I think you two might be switching rooms."

"Is Greece cursed or something?" Griffin asked.

Jordan popped out of the bathroom in a gray T-shirt and flannel pants. She looked at Noah.

"A little bonding will do you good. I'll go hang with Maggie and see you in the morning, okay?"

"No," he said, wanting her to hear the apology in his voice, since the word "sorry" itself didn't cut it. "It's not okay."

"I love you," she said. "Let's just sleep on this." Then she slipped past Griffin and out the door.

Griffin dug his hands into the front pockets of his jeans.

"So," he said with a pained smile. "You wanna be the big spoon or the little one?"

Noah closed his eyes and took a deep breath. He opened them at the sound of the door clicking shut, and then narrowed his gaze at his new roommate.

"I'm the whole freaking drawer of silverware, Reed. But you're welcome to the couch."

They both turned toward what could only be described as a loveseat, and a miniature one at that.

Griffin shrugged. "Works for me." He walked over to what was about to become his makeshift bed and collapsed onto one of the cushions and crossed his arms. "So, are we, like, supposed to talk about our feelings and solve each other's problems and shit?" he asked.

Noah opened the drawer in the dresser that housed the extra linens and then grabbed a pillow from the bed, chucking the whole pile at Griffin.

"Nope," Noah said.

Griffin nodded. "I like the way you think. But can I offer one piece of advice?"

Noah shook his head. "You're going to give it to me anyway, though. Right?"

Griffin smiled. "Looks like you got me all figured out, Keating. All I'm going to say is this—don't hide anything from her. Put it all out there, all your cards on the table. That's the only way she's going to know how you really feel, and it's the only way she's going to trust that even when you fuck up, you really do love her and want her to go to Washington with you because a year without her, even if it means chasing a dream, will be a fucking nightmare."

Noah ran a hand through his hair.

"Are you drunk?" he asked.

"Maybe a little. I had a couple drinks and considered sleeping in the lobby when I decided this might be the less humiliating of the two choices."

Noah couldn't help it. He laughed.

"How are you feeling about your choice right now?" he asked.

Griffin pursed his lips. "Jury's still out."

Noah leaned on the edge of the bed.

"I'll tell her how I feel," he said. "But I'm not sure that's enough to fix me ruining our engagement."

Griffin hissed in a breath. "How'd you do that?"

Noah sighed. "By just being me," he said.

He reached for the lamp on the side table and clicked it off. Then he sank down onto the bed, still in his clothes but too wiped out to give a shit.

"You should take your own advice," he told Griffin. "Sounds like you still have a lot to say to Maggie."

Noah listened as Griffin positioned himself on what had to be the worst excuse for a bed, but he guessed it was a step above the lobby.

"Wise words," Griffin said. "Wise words."

Noah chuckled and closed his eyes.

"Good talk, Keating," Griffin added through a yawn.

"Good talk, Reed."

And it kind of was, though Noah was sure neither would admit it to anyone outside that room.

Chapter Twenty-Two

MAGGIE

Jet lag had finally won, and Maggie was more than willing to succumb. Her will was nothing against the weight of her eyelids. So what if she didn't know where Griffin had been for the past hour or if he was coming back.

"I need to clear my head," he'd told her after they walked back to the hotel. Maggie had known Greece would be an adventure, but she couldn't have anticipated a journey that started with her and Griffin—the whole future in their hands—and would end with them poised for a year apart.

Ugh. The more she thought about it, the heavier her heart became. It was as if it had to work harder to beat against the ache. How would they enjoy whatever time they had left when she knew he was leaving?

Her eyes were open again, and she fought to shut out the world, or at least the room she was supposed to share with the man she loved. Instead she was curled up on her side alone, her body the perfect shape to fit against his, but Griffin wasn't there.

A knock sounded on the door, and for a second her heart raced until she remembered Griffin had his room key. Who the hell was here at this time of night?

Maggie trudged to the door and rested her eye against the peephole.

Miles winked, as if he could see her peering at him. He was still in his clothes from the plane, and Maggie realized she hadn't heard from him since he'd texted hours ago about being with Alex.

She threw open the door, ready to launch the inquisition, when she found Jordan standing next to him.

"Okay. What's going on?" Maggie asked.

Miles crossed his arms and nodded at Jordan. "You first," he said. "I have a feeling this is going to be interesting."

Jordan bit her lip. "Ummm…since Griffin is crashing with Noah, I thought I might crash here?"

"Griffin's crashing with Noah?" Miles asked.

"On your engagement night?" Maggie added. At least she knew where he was now, and that he was safe.

Miles's eyes widened. "I missed an engagement?" He grabbed Jordan's hand and put the other on Maggie's shoulder, nudging one girl backward as he tugged the other into the room with him. "We need a pint of Ben and Jerry's or something. Do they sell that here?"

Maggie walked to a large gift basket sitting on the dresser.

"No ice cream," she said. "But we have whatever's in here." She rummaged through the various wrapped but obviously homemade treats that had been left for all the out-of-towners at the check-in desk. "These look like a great way to eat our feelings, yes?" Maggie held up a cellophane-covered plate of what looked like small snowballs.

"Shit," Miles whispered, and Maggie raised her brows.

"Spill it, Parker. Sounds like you have some feelings that

need to be eaten, too."

Miles snatched the goodies from her outstretched hand and carried the plate to the bed where he kicked off his shoes and positioned himself cross-legged next to the girls.

"These…" Miles removed the wrapping from the plate and popped one of the small snowballs into his mouth. His eyes fluttered shut, and he groaned. "Are *Kourabiedes*."

Maggie and Jordan just stared as the man in front of them seemed to have some sort of sensual experience with the food in his mouth.

"Jesus, Miles," Maggie said. "It's just a cookie."

His eyes flew open.

"*Just* a cookie? Just a *cookie*, Mags? Taste one. Both of you get over here and taste one."

Maggie and Jordan couldn't help but obey. These were apparently some important cookies. They joined him on the bed, and each popped one of the small treats in her mouth.

Jordan let out a long, "Mmmmm," while Maggie's expression betrayed nothing of what she felt.

"You're kidding me, right?" Miles asked. "You don't like it?"

Maggie shook her head. "It's not that."

Ugh. Obviously both Miles and Jordan needed some sort of comfort of their own. Why else would they have shown up? But Maggie was in no position to make someone *else* feel better when she felt so crappy herself.

"Hey," Miles said, his voice soft and gentle, as if he'd heard her inner monologue and knew that whatever he needed her for, maybe right now she needed him a little bit more. "It's okay, Mags." He grabbed her hand between his and kissed her knuckles. "Whatever it is, we'll fix it."

Maggie pressed her lips together and forced a smile while Jordan popped another cookie into her mouth.

"I'm listening," Jordan said. "Just burying my emotions in

powdered sugar." She squeezed Maggie's knee. "How about you go first, then, Miles?"

"Like a circle of sharing or something?" he asked. "I dig it." He rose and padded over to the dresser until he found whatever he was looking for. Then he joined the two girls on the bed again. "Here." He handed Maggie a miniature bottle of ouzo. "Like *Lord of the Flies*. Our own version of the conch shell. Whoever has the ouzo has the floor. All others shall remain quiet."

Jordan held up a third cookie. "Sucks to your ass-mar!" Then she popped it into her mouth.

Miles narrowed his eyes at her.

"Sorry," Jordan said. "Couldn't help it. Maggie has the conch."

"Fine," Maggie said. "I'll do this on one condition. No advice or trying to solve anyone else's problems until we've all had the floor to air our grievances."

"This is very official," Miles said. "I like it."

And then Maggie started from the beginning—from coming home a mess the other night, to Griffin not only keeping the letter from her but not telling her he was applying for the fellowship in the first place, to Maggie telling him she couldn't move to Washington. As soon as she finished, Miles opened his mouth to speak, but Maggie shook her head.

"You aren't holding the conch yet, and I'm not quite done with it."

She unscrewed the top and took a tiny sip, really only for the purpose of ceremony. Then she closed it back up and handed it to Miles.

"No comments on my story," she told him. "Only *your* story. And then you drink and pass it to Jordan."

He accepted the bottle without hesitation.

"Deal," he said. "But I'm going out of order." He took his sip before he spoke. "Liquid courage," he added. "May not be much, but it's more than I had thirty seconds ago."

Jordan narrowed her eyes. "There better be enough left for me, mister."

He shook the bottle so she could hear the liquid slosh around.

"Now zip it while I have the conch."

Jordan made a motion of zipping her lips and throwing away the key, and for the first time that evening, Maggie laughed. Sure, life was one big ball of suck right now, but these two people—an old friend and maybe a new one, too—could get her to smile in spite of it.

"I think I'm maybe, possibly, falling for a guy I met this morning. *The* guy, by the way, who has made it possible for us to eat our feelings this evening—thank you, Alex. And I don't know what's worse—the fact that in mere hours this guy has broken down every barrier I put up for the past few years or that I don't think I can stop this train from flying right off the tracks by the end of this weekend."

He held up the bottle, studying it with his brows furrowed.

"Just drink it," Jordan said.

She winked at him, and he didn't waste a second, the bottle opened and drained almost before she finished speaking.

"I've been waiting *years* to get the dirt on you," Maggie said, knowing it wasn't easy for Miles to open up and wondering what brought on the change.

"I do owe you some history here. And I guess you both get to weigh in now." Miles leaned back against the headboard and crossed and uncrossed his arms. Maggie had never seen him anything other than in control. That's why she loved him so much. He was her best friend. Her rock. But she'd never realized that maybe all this time Miles needed his own rock, too.

"I've never been ashamed or afraid to be who I am," he continued. "I enjoy sex with a man as much as I do a woman.

I fall for a person's inner beauty as much as what's on the outside, and that should go for everyone. And *maybe* my options are a little broader than someone who only likes men or only likes women, but fuck. I've never had to apologize or defend who I was…until Cole."

Maggie raised her hand, and Miles chuckled.

"Yes, Maggie?"

She held out her hand and stared pointedly at the empty bottle in his. He relinquished it.

"My little rule follower," he said, and she narrowed her eyes.

"The floor is mine, now, Mr. Parker, mainly because I need a second to ask—who the hell is Cole, and can I virtually kick his ass for making you feel like you are anything other than spectacular?"

Miles snatched the bottle back. Jordan's eyes followed the action as if she were watching a tennis match.

"Cole happened before I met you. And it wasn't like you think. Not at first. Cole knew I was bi. But he'd only ever dated gay men before. And it was fine in the beginning. Pretty fucking fantastic, actually. Then I'd notice a beautiful woman— just look at her—and he would accuse me of switching sides. If I checked out a guy, he'd tell me to just come out already and be done with it." He scrubbed a hand over his face, then through his hair.

Maggie knew what was coming next. She should have always known, that Miles was Miles not just because he liked to keep things light and fun. Miles was Miles because someone had broken his heart, had made him feel like he couldn't be himself and be loved at the same time.

Maggie raised her hand again, and Jordan grabbed the empty ouzo bottle from Miles.

"I'm starting to think the whole *Lord of the Flies* theme maybe isn't appropriate for our sad love stories. Plus, I don't think Maggie here can hold her tongue anymore. I hereby retire the conch and give everyone in this room permission to speak freely. All those in favor, eat another cookie."

All three reached for the plate at the same time. But Maggie couldn't wait the span of time it would take to chew *and* swallow, so she spoke as soon as she could.

"You loved him. Didn't you?" she asked, and Miles nodded. "But he couldn't handle the bi thing." Again, another nod. "Okay," she continued. "Pep talk time, if it's okay to do before Jordan's turn."

Jordan nodded earnestly, so Maggie went on.

"*Cole* couldn't handle you being bi, sweetie. But that was *his* problem, not yours. I'm sorry he broke your heart. What's worse is he made you believe that other people would feel the same as he did. But you are one of the most beautiful, loving people I know. Who you have the potential to fall in love with has nothing to do with your capacity to be faithful, and you *know* that."

But Maggie wasn't a stranger to insecurity or the way fear of the unknown could warp your perception. Miles was one of the strongest, most confident people she knew. At least, that's what he'd let her see. Now she understood that they all wore masks at one time or another, not necessarily lies but only sharing one version of the truth.

"But, honey," she continued, "keeping everyone at a distance for years is one hell of a lonely place to be. I know. I invented that game. But if you don't risk your heart again—if you don't trust that someone can love you for your heart and soul no matter what—then it's worse than getting it broken because it'll never be quite whole. Not all by itself."

Jordan sighed. "Noah's heart makes mine whole."

Maggie smiled. "Yeah. Griffin makes mine whole, too."

Miles groaned. "Then why are you two here and your *You complete me*s down the hall?"

"Because Griffin broke my trust in him. And he's leaving for a year," Maggie told him.

"And Noah asked me to marry him in front of everybody *only* after Duncan spilled the beans and congratulated me on the engagement that hadn't happened yet. And you know what? It was beautiful and perfect...until he told me he wished it hadn't happened. That it wasn't supposed to be like that."

Miles whacked his head against the headboard.

"Mags...go with him. You have *nothing* keeping you in Minneapolis." Maggie opened her mouth to protest, but Miles held up his hand. "And Jordan, did he rescind his offer?" Jordan shook her head. "Then maybe he had something else planned that he didn't get to do. Maybe he thinks he could have done better. You guys are traveling after this, right? Maybe he wanted to do it where you first met, with the perfect words in the most perfect moment. Like, what if he had some amazing speech, where he planned to tell you how you're the wind beneath his wings, that you complete him, and that his heart cannot go on without you?"

Jordan snorted. "Did you just sum up our relationship with *Beaches*, *Jerry Maguire*, and *Titanic*?"

Miles shrugged. "Who am I to deny the power of Bette Midler, Tom Cruise, and Celine Dion? Take it from a guy who, for a long time, thought he was responsible for his own broken heart. The fear of losing someone is a very powerful thing. If Noah blames himself for any pitfalls in your past, he probably saw this as his one chance to get it right, and Duncan kind of took that away from him."

Jordan pulled her knees to her chest. "He's not going to lose me," she argued.

Miles shrugged. "Maybe he doesn't get that yet. Give him the chance to show you in *his* way that you're his eternal flame, that every little thing you do is magic."

"Stop it," Jordan said, but she was laughing.

"I'm sure he's hopelessly devoted to you."

Jordan kicked him playfully. "Enough. I get it. He loves me but needs to prove something to himself, even if I don't need him to prove it to me."

Miles laughed. "If you need a wedding playlist, I'm your guy."

Maggie narrowed her eyes at him. "If you think it's so easy for us, why can't it be easy for you?" she asked.

He crossed his arms. "First of all, I wasn't supposed to even be here. I'm an add-on to this whole wedding shindig. An afterthought. I wasn't supposed to fucking *fall* for someone in the midst of all this." He let out a long breath. "Do either of your men live more than an ocean away? Who falls in love and commits to something like that? I…I have a thesis to finish and defend."

Maggie nudged his foot with hers. "And after that? You don't have anyone or anything tying to you Minneapolis after May. You could risk your heart and be in love *anywhere.*"

Both girls nodded at him, and Maggie was grateful for Jordan's solidarity. But she also knew that Miles's own words, the ones she was echoing to him now, had a lot of merit.

The only people Maggie had in Minneapolis were Griffin and Miles. She'd always just assumed that the safe little bubble she'd let these two men into would never burst. But after tonight, it was starting to leak. Eventually it would deflate, and she would have to step outside the safety zone—but not at the expense of Griffin's peace of mind. This fellowship in D.C. was an amazing opportunity for him. How would he be able to enjoy it, to put the work into it that would make him successful, if he was always worrying about her? That was the part she couldn't let go of.

Miles brushed the powdered sugar from the bedspread and made sure the cookies were carefully stowed on the night table. Then he hopped off the bed and patted the spot where he'd just been.

"How about you ladies spoon it out?"

Maggie's brows drew together. "Where are you going?"

He put on that patented Miles grin, the one that told her he was up to no good but would enjoy every second of being bad.

"I told Alex I was coming back for my bag and to have a quick shower. He's probably already thinking I decided to cut and run—which, to be honest, was exactly what I was doing here."

Maggie stood as well, wrapping her arms around her friend in a tight embrace.

"Open yourself up to possibility, sweetie," she whispered in his ear. "Don't let someone who couldn't love you like you deserve keep you from someone who can."

He squeezed her back, and she felt his heart hammering against her.

"Don't tell anyone, Mags," he whispered back to her, "but I'm scared."

"We all are," she assured him before pulling away and kissing him on the forehead. "Text me when you get there so I know you made it safe. I don't like you walking back there alone so late."

Miles winked. "You got it, darling." He turned to Jordan, and Maggie followed his gaze. "Good night—" He stopped before uttering her name, and Maggie giggled as they both found Jordan passed out on top of the bedspread, head on a pillow and a smudge of powdered sugar on her nose.

"She's going to be okay, right? I mean, her and Noah?" Maggie asked.

Miles nodded. "So are you and Griffin," he said. "It's okay to be scared, but it's not okay to let fear take the wheel."

"Wise words from a man who let fear drive him all the

way to my room tonight."

Miles chuckled. "Touché. I'm taking the wheel now. Maybe you should, too."

And then he kissed her on the cheek and was out the door before she could respond.

Maggie crawled into bed next to Jordan. She had to tug, jostling her bedmate, to loosen the linens enough so she could climb under the sheets. It didn't matter. Jordan was out cold.

But Maggie lay awake for a while longer, trying to convince herself that her reasons for not wanting to go to Washington were rational and not born of her own fear. Because Miles was right. There was nothing holding her in Minneapolis except for the safety of routine.

What if she had to learn a new routine? Would she be able to adapt, or would it set her back the three years it had taken her to get where she was now?

Maggie wanted to know the answer, but right now she was losing the battle. Sheer will was nothing against a monster case of jet lag, and as elusive as it had been before Miles and Jordan showed up, sleep finally came. Her last thought was a projection into her near future—rolling over in the bed she shared with Griffin to find his side empty, his nightstand devoid of his glasses and whatever book he was reading.

And *that*? Well, that was the scariest thought of all.

Chapter Twenty-Three

DUNCAN

Duncan's fist pounded against Noah's door, but there was no answer. He checked his phone again. Seven o'clock. Fucking hell, what was he doing awake at a time such as this? Oh, right.

"I'm getting married today, ya bastard! Wake up and have a pint with me, aye? I'll just go call on Griffin and be right back." He turned to make his way farther down the hall to Griffin's room when he remembered his slight oversight.

He knocked again.

"And mornin' to ya, too, Jordan. I'm sorry if I woke—"

Before he could finish, the door swung open to reveal Griffin standing in nothing but his jeans. Duncan didn't have time to process what he was seeing because he was more concerned with the brain malfunction that had led him to believe he was at one location when really he was at another. He hadn't had that much to drink last night, and even if he had, his talk with Elaina helped fast-forward him to complete and total sobriety.

"Jesus. What time is it?"

The question came from behind Griffin, and though he didn't know her well, Duncan was sure Maggie hadn't grown a set of baws overnight.

Griffin pulled the door wide, and Duncan's eyes took in his surroundings—a blanket and pillow on the couch, the hotel bed unmade just enough to fit one body along the outer edge.

"Aw hell, lads. What did ya do?" Duncan asked. "I thought I was the only one who fucked up last evening." He nodded to them both. "You, too?"

Griffin scrubbed a hand across his jaw and looked toward Noah.

Noah shook his head slowly.

"What?" Duncan asked. "Out with it. It's my wedding day—if the bride will still have me, though now she thinks I won't have her, which is ridiculous, though I did have a bit of a freak-out—shite! What the fuck was I saying? Right. Why are you two here…*together*?"

Noah was acting all cagey, scratching the back of his neck, and Duncan didn't like it. Not one bit. He narrowed his eyes at the two of them.

"Awright, mates. Someone is going to come clean, right about…now. Let's have it."

"I got this," Noah said to Griffin before turning back to Duncan. "See…Duncan…I wasn't actually going to propose to Jordan last night. I had this whole idea of doing it on the train to Scotland—or maybe even on campus. But—this weekend was yours. I had no intention of overshadowing that."

Duncan's brows pulled together. "Overshadowing? I don't— I mean I didn't— Wait—" It was all clicking into place. His stomach did this twisting thing that made him feel like the morning after a bottle of Drambuie. But instead of getting sick, his stomach held on to its meager contents, and the man himself slumped against the back of the door.

"I announced the engagement before it happened."

Noah nodded. "But it's my fault Jordan's not here, Duncan. Not yours. *I* messed up."

Duncan's eyes met Griffin's, and he finally saw the sadness there.

"Aw, shite, Griffin. I told Maggie you were going away." Duncan slid all the way down to the floor now, half laughing and half wincing. "Guys—I don't know what to say. I wasn't myself yesterday. It was all just too much. And now I'm afraid I may have ruined the day for all of us."

Griffin turned and walked back toward the couch, grabbing his phone off the nearby dresser.

"Enough," he said, eyes on the screen as he scrolled for something with his thumb.

"Enough what?" Duncan asked, arms draped over his knees and his chin sunk all the way to his chest.

And then he heard it, that unmistakable electric guitar rhythm. As much as he wanted to mope, Duncan lifted his head. Griffin was smiling, head nodding to the beat.

"Dude," Noah said, laughing. "You are fucking out of your mind."

"Get up, McAllister," Griffin commanded.

Duncan stood. He couldn't *not*. And once he was up, he couldn't keep his head from bobbing in time with the music, either. Aw hell, he was almost dancing, and he hadn't even had a pint yet.

"You just happen to have 'Eye of the Tiger' ready and waiting on your playlist?" Noah asked, and Griffin's smile grew. He held out his phone for Noah to see.

"A man never knows when he may need the help of one of the greatest American bands from the eighties. It's like a pep talk from Rocky Balboa each time!"

"Mickey gives the pep talks, asshole," Noah said, but he was still laughing.

All of them were laughing.

Duncan had made a right mess of everything, starting with the Athens airport. He'd just thought he needed a few minutes to clear his head, to get used to his new life. And now he had to save that new life before it wasn't his anymore. And he had to make sure Griffin and Noah did the same.

He opened the door.

"Where are you going?" Noah asked, but Duncan shook his head.

"We," he said. "We are going down to the lobby for a pint, and then we're going to fix everything."

Noah shrugged. "I could use a pint." He slipped on his shoes and joined Duncan at the door.

"Early-morning pints it is," Griffin added and stepped toward the two other men.

Duncan held up his hand to halt any further movement.

"Put on a shirt, ya bastard. That may work on your Maggie, but I want none of it."

Griffin brandished his phone.

"Sticks and stones, my friend. Got my soundtrack," Griffin said, backtracking toward the couch and collecting his shirt from the floor. "Let's do this. Pints, kilts, and romantic gestures sure to repair the damage we've done."

"I'll drink to that," Noah said, following Duncan out into the hall.

"What romantic gestures?" Duncan asked.

"That's what we need to figure out," Griffin said.

And with that he was the last to exit the room, letting the door fall closed behind him.

Chapter Twenty-Four

MILES

Okay, so maybe Miles felt slightly like Edward Cullen at the moment, watching Alex sleep, but he couldn't help it. He'd woken only to take a piss, but as he padded back to the bed, he noticed how, in sleep, Alex's full lips parted just enough to let air pass between them. It was also hard to miss the lulling cadence of his chest rising and falling with each rhythmic breath. And really, what man could ignore how the rumpled bedsheet had slid down just past that delicious hip bone? Miles knew—he'd licked that hip bone.

It wasn't a matter of opinion. No. This was undeniable fact. Alex was the most beautiful human he had ever encountered, and he'd be damned if he was going to take his eyes off him so long as he was awake.

"I can feel you staring."

The deep morning rasp of Alex's voice did nothing to calm what stirred inside Miles's belly—and a little farther south. His eyes dipped to where his boxer briefs hid nothing, and Miles laughed quietly to himself. Who *was* this man, and what had he done with Miles's boundaries, with the safety net that surrounded his heart?

"I can feel you feeling me staring," Miles said. "And I'm not gonna lie—it's, uh, *doing* things to me."

At this Alex cocked an eye open, just one. But it was enough to see Miles ready and willing inside his briefs.

"Get back in this bed immediately," Alex demanded. "I want my fill of you before I have to work the rest of the day and night."

Miles didn't waste a second. He nearly dove into the bed. Because he wanted his fill, too. The only problem was, he didn't think there was enough time to satiate his need.

Alex's eyes were closed again, but he was smiling. Then Miles realized the man was waiting. It was *his* move; Miles was to take the lead. But a feeling, long foreign to him, took over what had initially brought him back to this bed. It wasn't the lust he thought he'd felt just by looking at Alex's barely covered body. It was…*loss.*

Miles was on some sort of precipice. He could *take his fill*, just as Alex would. He could keep up the fantasy and never let Alex know more than he did right now.

That would be safe—typical Miles. But safe hadn't introduced him to happiness yet. Sharing only pieces of his true self hadn't made him whole. So it was time for another approach.

"I want to tell you something—something more than my name," Miles said, and Alex opened both eyes, then rose up on his elbow to face his bed partner.

"I like women," Miles started, and Alex didn't flinch. "I like women, and I like men, too."

Alex dragged his teeth across his bottom lip, the action simple enough—one Miles had seen at least a hundred people perform before, and he would see hundreds do it again. But all he wanted was to see Alex do it. Alex's teeth on Alex's sexy, pouty bottom lip.

Miles's mouth went dry, and he knew what he wanted — what he *needed* — to alleviate the drought.

"Tell me…" Alex started, and it didn't matter what came next. Miles would tell this man whatever he wanted to hear. And then Alex smiled, as if he knew he had Miles exactly where he wanted him. "Are you thinking about women right now?"

Alex let his palm fall on Miles's inner thigh, his thumb teasing at the hem of his briefs.

"No," Miles said, taking care not to breathe in too deeply — or out for that matter — fearing a sudden movement would upset this suspended animation they seemed to be in. And as much as he wanted to obliterate any space left between them, he would not escape this moment. No more easy way out. If only for a short weekend, Miles was going to let go. He was going to let this man know everything, to give himself over to possibility.

And then he would leave.

Alex's palm took to massaging his thigh, the movement slow and deliberate and completely maddening. Then that rogue thumb brushed right over his balls, and Miles hissed in a breath. This guy wasn't playing fair.

"How about other men?" Alex asked, his voice like melted chocolate that Miles would willingly lap up. "Are you thinking about other men?" Alex wasn't asking these questions out of jealousy. Miles could hear that in his voice, in the reassurance and confidence of his tone. Alex *knew* that in this moment Miles wanted only him. It wasn't Alex who lacked trust. It was him.

If spontaneous combustion in humans did, in fact, exist, Miles was sure it was caused by the voice of one Alexander Karas. And *maybe* the tips of his fingers had something to do with it, too.

Miles placed a palm on Alex's cheek, and he felt skin as hot as fire. He ran a thumb over that bottom lip, the one that was demanding to be kissed, and Alex licked the tip of Miles's thumb.

"I swear to the fucking gods on Mount Olympus…" Miles said. "That since you sat down next to me on the plane, I have thought of no one but you. I have wanted no one but you. And if I had my way, I would have no one but you for as long as you'd let me."

He didn't wait for a response but instead pulled Alex to him, using only enough restraint so as not to devour the man whole.

Teeth grazed skin, and tongues danced in a kiss so wild and full of passion that Miles knew for certain if this were another place or time, this would be the person he'd fall for— the one who would see all of him and still want him.

Alex slid his hand up inside the leg of Miles's briefs, cupping and massaging and teasing that space between front and back. Everything inside Miles twisted and tangled in agonizing pleasure. Alex's hand left him for an excruciating few seconds, the time it took to remove Miles's underwear completely.

"It was getting in the way," Alex whispered against his neck as he kissed him on the collarbone as Miles lay bare.

An open book ready for reading.

Alex stroked Miles from root to tip, his thumb swirling the wetness, and Miles knew the answer to the unanswered question, to the one thing that would send him over the edge with no chance of making it back.

"Yes," Miles said. "I want you inside me."

Alex kissed him, hard at first and then whisper-soft, both hungry and gentle. Ever since Alex asked for an all-access weekend pass, something shifted. Miles knew that letting him in would be too much.

But Alex knew. And still wanted him. Miles had almost let him in already.

Alex led him from the bed to his shower, where they washed away any barriers left between them, a wordless cleansing of all the thoughts that had kept Miles from considering a moment like this.

Back in Alex's bed, there was no more need for consideration. He rolled Miles to his side and pulled him to his chest. His hand traveled the length of Miles's torso, fingers swirling in the fine hair that dusted his chest, following the narrow trail to where he was long and rigid and pulsing with need.

Alex prepared him gently, his fingers slick with lubrication, driving him mad yet only making him want *more*. Again the tease and then the departure, but Miles laughed when he heard Alex rummaging through the nightstand drawer. Seconds later he felt Alex's length against his back and then heard the sound of foil tearing.

Alex kissed his neck, warm breath tickling Miles's skin.

"All dressed up and someplace incredible to go," Alex said, and Miles chuckled. Then Alex wrapped his hand around him again, nudging him open from behind and entering with ease.

"Jesus," Miles gasped, reaching back to tangle his fingers in Alex's hair.

"What happened to swearing on the Olympians?" Alex asked, and Miles's chest shook with silent laughter and a bliss like he'd never known.

"Fucking hell," Miles groaned as Alex pulled out halfway and sunk in to the hilt, all the while stroking Miles from bottom to top. "Whatever or whoever you want me to swear to, consider myself sworn."

Alex rocked against him, his hand never missing a beat,

though Miles was sure his heart skipped at least one or two. He ran a hand down Alex's leg, feeling the long scar that spanned the length from his knee to his shin. Alex had shared with him an event that altered his life, and Miles wondered if today could be one that altered his. He craned his neck to find those lips he craved, whispering to Alex as he did.

"You're in," Miles said just as Alex thrust deep, and his eyes rolled to the back of his head as Alex hit that perfect spot inside. He wondered if Alex understood, if he'd even heard him at all, or if he was now too caught up in coming so close to the edge.

Alex slowed the rhythm of his body yet pumped Miles's length harder. Close. He was so close, every part of him a pinprick away from combustion.

"You're in as well," Alex said, and those were the last words Miles heard before total oblivion.

Alex had more than understood. He'd felt it, too.

Miles lay watching the beautiful man next to him doze for "just five more minutes" before the day truly began.

This couldn't be real because no one fell this fast. Miles would roll his eyes at anyone who said otherwise. Yet here he was, wondering how getting his heart broken all those years ago could even compare to saying good-bye to Alex.

And then there was that familiar, niggling feeling. The one he knew would rear its ugly head eventually. He may have let Alex past his barriers, but tomorrow he could construct them again.

Relief. That's what the lightness he felt was. As much as he let his guard down, Miles had an impenetrable safe zone. It was called home.

Greece wasn't real. It was fantasy, and he could live in

this fantasy world for a few more hours. But no matter what Alex told him this morning, tonight, tomorrow—it would all change if they tried to do this for the long haul, and Miles had the scars to prove it.

"I've got to get dressed for the ceremony," he said, kissing Alex softly on the mouth.

Alex let out a groggy, "Mmmmmm," against Miles's lips as he kissed him back. "As soon as the serving begins tonight," Alex told him, "I'm officially off duty, and don't think I won't steal you away as soon as humanly possible."

"I'm planning on it," Miles said. Because he was. And because he knew good-bye would be the hardest to bear, he also planned on being gone before Alex woke in the morning.

Chapter Twenty-Five

Elaina finally kicked everyone out of her room. Her makeup was done, and the dress was on. Holy shit, the dress. Elaina wasn't one for false modesty, and since no one else was in the room, she admitted to herself that she did look spectacular. The dress had been her mother's—and her grandmother's before that. Now she stood in awe of the person in the mirror, wrapped in history in the hopes of embarking on her future.

She ran her fingertips over the scalloped neckline, the ivory lace bodice like a glove against her skin. The A-line skirt and train were classic elegance, easy enough to sit in and sure not to trip her as she glided down the aisle. The only question was whether or not there'd be a groom at the other end to greet her.

Someone knocked softly on the door, and Elaina groaned. No more cousins, grandmothers, mothers, friends. Enough. She just wanted a few moments of peace before she faced what would either be her best day—or her worst.

She took a step toward the door and then with a haughty upturn of her chin spun the other way. She had always been good at avoiding anyone or anything she didn't want to deal with. The thought made her chuckle. Duncan had been one such person a few years ago. He'd made his interest in her clear from the start, and despite his dark, sexy hair and eyes—not to mention those lean, muscular legs in a kilt—she tried not to give in to her attraction.

Elaina could excuse her silly judgment then. She was, after all, only a student who thought she had everything figured out, especially the kind of *man* she wanted in her life. Certainly no boy who, on occasion, drank his weight in whisky and woke up the next morning on a roundabout would fit her narrow definition. Not a boy who favored hours in front of a PlayStation over a good book. *Not* that Elaina was a prolific reader, but a man who read was, well, a man, right?

She slumped into the chair in front of her dressing table. Duncan may enjoy his liquor as well as his video games, but he also graduated with some of the highest marks at Aberdeen. Her father trusted him enough to offer him a job and to give his blessing on their marriage after they'd been dating for less than a year.

"I am a terrible human," she mumbled to herself.

And then the knocking came again.

Suffused with new anger, she stormed to the door.

"Ten minutes!" she yelled, ready to unleash her fury on who was surely Thea, wanting to do a last-minute touch-up before they left for the church. "I want ten freaking minutes to myself before…" She threw the door open, yelped, and then promptly jumped behind it, shielding herself from view.

"Hiya to you as well," Duncan said, and she could hear that devil of a smile. "You sure are a sight, Elaina. Though I only saw ya for a wee second."

Elaina burrowed farther into the corner between the wall and the open door.

"What the hell are you doing here?" But she couldn't help it. She was smiling. For the first time since Duncan had arrived in Greece, Elaina Tripoli felt something she hadn't thought was there. Hope.

"May I come in? We've already had one conversation like this, and I think I'd like to have this one face-to-face," he said.

"But you are not supposed to see the bride. It is very bad luck."

The door moved slowly toward her, and she knew Duncan was waiting for her to stop it, to refuse his entrance, but how could she refuse the man she thought she might not see again after last night?

"Elaina," he said, stepping into the room and closing the door so she stood in plain sight, bad luck be damned.

He opened his mouth to continue speaking, but nothing came out. His right palm flew to his heart, and he pressed his lips together, holding back…*something*. So Elaina waited until he was ready.

Duncan cleared his throat, and she tried not to notice that his eyes shone a bit more than they had last night, brimming with emotion she'd not seen from him before. Though his eye was still bruised, it was no longer swollen, and she let him drink her in, holding her breath as he did. He stepped toward her, where she was still pinned to the corner, more by sheer paralysis than anything else.

"I think we make our own luck, aye?" he said, taking her hand in his, and Elaina felt him trembling. Then he brought her palm to his lips and pressed a small kiss there.

"I don't deserve you, Duncan."

She moved her palm to his cheek, and he leaned into it. Deserving or not, right there, in that one gesture, Elaina knew he was hers and she his.

"Aye," he said. "Ya sell yourself too short, love. I'm plenty responsible, in my own way, for what happened yesterday. And I don't blame you for being angry."

He pulled her hand to his chest, and it was only then that Elaina's eyes were able to focus on the man who stood before her. She'd seen him in his kilt before, but a T-shirt or jumper had always accompanied it. He was the one who was a sight.

"Oh, Duncan. Look at you."

He grinned, and though his heart hammered against her hand, she felt it slow to an even rhythm.

"You're not mad about the eye?" His smile faltered with the question. "It'll be in all the photos."

She reached for his face with her free hand, letting her thumb brush over the bruise.

"You're beautiful," she told him. "This happened because of what you did for me, and I won't forgive myself for thinking otherwise."

He took both her wrists in his hands and lowered her arms to her sides. "We have to be done with the apologies and blame, Elaina. I'm here to marry you, dammit. It's time to move forward. Promise me that from this moment on, we leave yesterday behind us because, fucking hell, I'd love to do that. It's the New Year tomorrow, after all. Let's start it with no regrets. Let's start it as husband and wife."

A smile tugged at her lips. That's what she was hoping for when the knock sounded on the door—to move forward. To start her future with the person she loved most.

"Step back and let me look at you, then," she told him, and he obliged.

Duncan raised his chin and tugged at the lapels of his navy jacket, preening for her.

"Ya like what ya see, aye."

She nodded. "Very much. Especially the socks." Okay, so maybe it wasn't the socks themselves she liked but the way they hugged his muscular calves. Duncan wasn't an athlete specifically, but he'd never owned a car. In the small part of Aberdeen where he'd grown up, he'd told Elaina he'd always loved walking. So by the time he was old enough to drive, he was in no rush to do so.

Duncan loved the outdoors, and Elaina loved the way it naturally sculpted his body.

"Actually," she amended, "I'd like to get you out of those socks. I would like to get you out of that entire gorgeous ensemble, but Thea will kill me if I ruin my makeup. And *I* will kill me if I ruin this dress."

Duncan held up a hand, hesitating for several seconds before letting his fingertips graze the neckline of her dress. She sucked in a sharp breath but didn't stop him.

"I don't have words, Elaina. Not the right ones to tell you what I see when I look at you."

"Try to tell me," she said, her voice barely above a whisper.

His fingers traced the scalloped neckline, each glide of his skin against hers sending ripples of goose bumps down her arms, her legs, her spine.

"It stops my heart, and not just because you're in that dress. Every day I see you and remind myself that you said yes, I lose a few seconds of my life." He inclined his head toward the exposed skin on her collarbone and kissed her once. Twice. Once more.

"Then call me heart-stopping," she squeaked out, her knees threatening to buckle.

"You're heart-stopping," he said, his lips continuing to follow the trail his fingers left. "And if I don't kiss you—because shite, Elaina, other than last night, it's been nearly a week—I'm not sure it'll start beating again."

She licked her lips, trying to remember what Thea had called the lipstick. A lip stain? *It's not supposed to rub off for hours,* she'd said.

Well. Time to put it to the test.

She grabbed him by his…purse or whatever you called that little pouch that hung over the front of his kilt, hiding one of Elaina's favorite parts of Duncan. She grinned and then crushed her mouth against his. And when his tongue slipped past her parted lips, she tasted his hunger—and his all-consuming love—and she fed off both.

"Marry me, Elaina Tripoli," he said against her lips, and oh how she loved the sound of those words.

"Yes," she replied. "My answer to that will always be yes."

He chuckled and kissed her again.

"What about after today, when you're my wife? I can't ask you to marry me then, can I?"

She ran her fingers through his hair, loving that he wore it longer these days. It gave her something to grab onto when she needed him closer, just as she did now.

"You can always ask me to be yours," she rasped against him. "And I'll *always* say yes." She gave his hair another soft tug.

He let out a quiet moan. "El-*ain*-a…" he pleaded. "We can't. Not now. I've got to sneak my arse out of here and see you at the church for the first time."

Her hands traveled to his neck, down the length of his back, then stopped to cup that lovely *varéli* through his kilt.

"Are you a *true* Scotsman?" she asked, and there was that delicious moan again. How she loved the things she could do to this man—and those he could do to her. Pity they couldn't do those things right now. She would test the boundaries of her lipstick, but with only minutes before she had to leave for the church, she was not about to push it any further.

Duncan stepped back and cupped her cheeks. Surely they were flushed far beyond explanation. She'd need a few minutes to cool down before her family saw her.

"I am a Scotsman, aye," he said. "But I am also a gentleman

when it's forty degrees and windy as hell. So you'll have to make do with my tartan knickers," he added, then proceeded to tease his wife-to-be by lifting his kilt just enough for her to see the McAllister tartan in undergarment form.

"Go," she said. "Go before I have my way with you and ruin my dress." She kissed him twice more—on the mouth and then on his beautiful and bruised cheek.

"There's nothing I want more than for you to have your way with me…but it will have to wait until you are Elaina McAllister, if that's okay with you."

She opened the door and pushed him through it. If she didn't, she'd never make it to becoming Elaina McAllister, but dammit she would enjoy the reason for missing her own wedding.

"I am not patient," she said. "Especially when it comes to you." And because she couldn't help herself, she put that lip stain to one final test. This kiss was soft yet expectant, and it would have to do until later. Much later. Shit.

"I love you," Duncan said, and then he slipped out the door without letting her respond, as if he didn't need to hear her reciprocate. As if he always knew that despite her inability to always show him how she really felt, he never doubted her.

Elaina would never, ever doubt this most beautiful man again.

I think we make our own luck, aye?

"Aye, Duncan," she said to herself. "I'm the luckiest person I know."

Chapter Twenty-Six

Maggie was already gone by the time Griffin had finished his pint with Duncan and Noah. She'd texted, though.

The bridal party is getting ready at Elaina's. Jordan said I could tag along.

Griffin's *Rocky* soundtrack came to a screeching halt. He'd been buoyed with confidence not only from his ridiculous playlist but from the other guys as well. They'd all gotten themselves into messes, yet each man had been well intentioned in doing so.

Yes, he should have told Maggie what he was doing from the start, and he shouldn't have put her in some virtual breakables cabinet. She was stronger than that, and he knew it. But that didn't stop him from wanting to protect her now and always. Nothing...*nothing* was more important to him than the girl who trusted him to be the man he'd always hoped he could be.

That was it—he had to convince her to trust him again, and with Maggie that meant only one thing: total and utter honesty about why he wasn't honest. Of course he would always worry about Maggie getting sick again, but that could happen anywhere. Her health wasn't the reason he'd kept the fellowship from her. He was scared of moving so far out of his safety zone in order to chase a dream he only realized he had once he met her, but that wasn't it, either. The biggest fear, the one that cost Griffin her trust, was that he didn't want any of it if it meant a life without her. It wasn't fair to put the responsibility for his happiness on her shoulders, not when she already carried so much. So he'd have to show Maggie that her burdens and responsibilities weren't hers alone anymore. That was the deal, the fine print on the contract of what it meant to love someone the way he loved her. It was time to lay his half of the deck on the table and hope that Maggie was all in, too.

NOAH

Noah found the small velvet box in his toiletry bag. He knew Jordan wouldn't be there when he returned. The bridal party was due at Elaina's at the same time he was having his morning pint. But his gut twisted at the sight of the ring back in his possession. Had he really fucked up this badly? If Jordan's *yes* was now a *no*, he wasn't sure he could take it. They'd come too far for him to have done irreparable damage. He had to believe that much because the alternative was unthinkable.

The whole point of this trip was to replace painful memories with positive ones, but that had already backfired.

Noah opened the box and found not just the ring but also a note.

Noah—

I wanted to wear it. I really did. But it felt strange. If last night wasn't how you wanted things to go, then I don't want to wear it...yet. This isn't just my moment. It's yours, too. And I should have realized that. I hope you know that I would say yes anywhere, anytime, as long as it was you asking. So I'll wait until it's right for you. I'm not going anywhere.

I love you.
Jordan

He bit the inside of his cheek and swallowed back the knot in his throat. *He* was supposed to be the one with the grand gesture, and here was Jordan Brooks, surprising him yet again. What had he done to deserve this beautiful, understanding, patient, perfect woman? And why the *hell* wasn't she here so he could take it all back, tell her he'd been ready since Scotland?

He called her cell. Right to voicemail.

Shit. Shit, shit, shit, shit, *shit.*

He'd see her at the church, but when or how could they talk? He wasn't going to propose to her while they were walking down the aisle. It was bad enough his first proposal stole the thunder from Duncan and Elaina's rehearsal dinner. He wasn't going to upstage the wedding as well.

The reception. He could do it at the reception. He *had* to do it before midnight. Noah would not start the New Year without his fiancée wearing her ring.

His phone buzzed with a text, and Noah saw Griffin's name on the screen.

Ready? Duncan has a taxi waiting.

Hell yes, he was ready. And this time he'd get everything right.

MILES

Miles straightened his tie and double-checked once more to make sure his pants were zipped. This was not the Miles Parker he'd cultivated for years. Nervous and unsure — those adjectives didn't suit him, yet here he was, suited up in formalwear and insecurity.

But damn. He *did* look good. That wasn't the issue. The issue was all these *feelings* — because Miles didn't *do* feelings. But he was having them anyway, which was ridiculous because he'd met Alex only yesterday.

Pull yourself together. He lives in Greece. And if he didn't, he'd be just like every other person you've dated who wanted to put you in a neat little box.

Gay. Straight. Those boxes couldn't contain him. It was easier to box up his heart than try to prove to any one lover that he was who he was.

Miles pulled on his jacket and took one last glance in the mirror. Nothing like a polished exterior to hide what's underneath. Maggie used to be the only person who could see right through him, but somehow Alex had gotten a glimpse of what lay beneath the surface. All it would take was a couple of drinks at the reception, and he could slip back into the persona everyone expected. He did many things well, and proving himself the life of the party was one of them, so that would be his role tonight. The life of the party never went home broken-hearted, right?

Tonight he was banking on that theory being true.

Chapter Twenty-Seven

DUNCAN

The Greek Orthodox ceremony, long as it was, felt like a blur. Somehow Duncan was standing in the church, face-to-face with Elaina, as the priest placed rings on the fingers of their right hands. A red carpet stretched down the whole aisle, and Duncan raised his head to take in the ornate murals painted along the ceiling. Before him stood his bride in ivory lace, her shoulders wrapped in the rich hue of the tartan scarf he'd fought so hard to save.

Duncan had never been anywhere like this place, and he'd never seen anyone as beautiful as the woman before him. It was something out of the colored pages of a history book, and now this would be a part of *his* history—and the start of his future. *Their* future.

Thea, Elaina's *Koumbara*, stepped forward on the priest's request and exchanged the rings three times. The next thing he knew, he was wearing a crown and sharing a cup of wine with his wife.

He needed a moment to collect himself, so he sipped slowly and watched as Elaina did the same. God, she was beautiful. Did he tell her that enough? Did she know that his breath caught at the sight of her, not just today but every time he looked at her and realized she'd chosen *him*? All of his fear and hesitation disintegrated into dust. Yesterday morning he'd seen a strange city that felt nothing like the only home he'd ever known. Today he saw a future, a family, a life he never knew he wanted, yet one he now cherished above everything else. Duncan hadn't chased that man through the airport to save a scarf. It was to save this—Elaina looking at him, loving him, bruises and all. He wasn't sure what he did to deserve this kind of happiness, but he'd spend the rest of his life grateful that he'd found it.

"We did it," he whispered, a catch in his voice he wasn't expecting.

Elaina promptly shushed him but then smiled, and he had to bite back a laugh. He would not ruin the solemnity of the ceremony. It was important to her to get married in the Greek church, and Duncan was happy to oblige. She wore a sixpence in her shoe and hid a sprig of white heather in her bouquet, both Scottish good luck charms. And the wedding scarf bore his family's tartan. At the moment, he couldn't ask for more, but when they got to the other end of the aisle? Well—he had plans.

The priest faced Duncan specifically. "Be magnified, O Bridegroom, as Abraham, and blessed as Isaac, and increased as was Jacob. Go your way in peace, performing in righteousness the commandments of God."

To Elaina he said, "And you, O Bride, be magnified as was Sarah, and rejoiced as was Rebecca, and increased as Rachel, being glad in your husband, keeping the paths of the Law, for so God is well pleased."

This was it. They were getting close. All that would be left after this would be to celebrate the first best day of his life.

One by one, the priest removed each crown before speaking his final words to the now married couple.

"Accept their crowns in Your Kingdom unsoiled and undefiled; and preserve them without offense to the ages of ages."

Duncan looked to his right and saw Griffin, Noah, and family members who made up the rest of the groomsmen in full McAllister tartan. To his left stood Thea and Jordan and many other cousins in various styled dresses, all in the same ruby hue as Elaina's scarf. Everyone he cared for was here, and the one he loved most was beside him, her hand in his, as the priest sent them forward.

Like a queen, *his* queen, Elaina glided down the aisle on his arm. He was her husband now. Her forever king. He had been wearing a crown, after all.

The entire congregation clapped as they made their way toward the exit. But just as they passed the last pew to the open, arched doorway, Duncan halted his step.

"What are you doing?" Elaina hissed under her breath as she nearly tripped over her wedding gown.

"Look up," he whispered, and she did. Elaina's eyes widened, and she broke into the most radiant grin he'd ever seen.

Mistletoe.

He'd remembered the Valentine's Day in Aberdeen when Elaina strung the plant all over the Blue Lantern, the pub where she worked. It had been her attempt to get Jordan and Noah back together, to hang the plant that encouraged snogging.

Right now, Duncan considered himself encouraged.

He wrapped his arm beneath his wife's shoulder blades and lowered her into a dramatic dip that preceded the long-awaited kiss.

Elaina didn't argue. She wrapped her arms around his neck and kissed him back.

And kissed him…and kissed him…and kissed him.

"Wait!" He pulled away from her, agonizing as it was. Something wasn't right.

Her brows furrowed as she straightened to meet his gaze. "What?" she hissed in as much of a whisper as she could. "Everyone is watching!"

He looked out at the congregation, silenced, no doubt, by the abrupt end to the couple's kiss. She was right. All eyes were on them.

Duncan held up his index finger, asking their audience to wait.

"There weren't vows. The priest didn't ask me if I take you to be mine."

Elaina rolled her eyes. "Father Markos explained the ceremony to you—the rings, crowns, prayers. We're married."

He nodded. "Aye. I just thought the vows came after all that. Just— Do you promise to love me always, forgive my messes, and trust that I'll always do right by you?"

At this, her eyes softened. And he saw out of his peripheral vision that congregants at the far end were starting to creep out of their pews, inching forward to listen to the impromptu second wedding that was happening under a sprig of mistletoe.

"Oh, Duncan," she said. "Of course I do."

He grinned. "Now ask me."

She bit her lip, smiling as well.

"Do you promise to love me always, forgive my tendency to be a *little* judgmental, and trust that I'll always do right by you?"

He grabbed both of her hands, kissing the top of each before turning toward their onlookers and shouting, "I do!"

Now everything felt right, and he wrapped his arms around her and kissed his bride again.

"I love you, Duncan McAllister." Her words were muffled by the catcalls of the wedding guests, but Duncan heard her, and that's all that mattered.

"And I love *you*, Elaina McAllister."

He took her hand in his, and they ran the rest of the way out of the church. They'd have to run right back in as soon as the place emptied—for an hour or two more of photographs—but for now they had a few quiet moments to themselves.

The sun shone bright, warming Duncan's face despite the cooler temperatures. In the distance he could see the parapets atop the cylindrical White Tower. Elaina's history. Their future.

He lifted her in his arms, kissing her as she slid down the length of his body and back to the ground. He felt five miles above the earth, though, and he didn't think he'd ever come down.

"Say it again," she said, and he grinned.

"I love you, Elaina McAllister." He kissed her cheek.

"Again," she whispered.

He kissed her chin. "Elaina…" And then her neck. "McAllister."

"Please," she started, and he could hear the shortness of her breath. "Don't ever stop."

He chuckled. "Kissing you or saying your new name?"

"Both," she said, taking his cheeks in her palms. "Both. Always."

Then her lips were on his, and Duncan wasn't sure he'd ever come back down to earth again.

The crowd erupted from the cathedral, and he knew he had just enough time for one more—for good measure.

He moved behind her so they both faced the entrance, wrapping his arms around her torso and kissing the exposed skin below her neck. "Elaina McAllister."

The roar of the crowd reached them at last. The rest of the day and night belonged to those who came to celebrate the happy couple, but tonight—tonight the king had plans for his queen.

Chapter Twenty-Eight

Jordan

All those hours together at the ceremony, and taking pictures after, and Noah had barely said a word to her. He'd readily linked his arm with hers for their walk down the aisle, but in all of the craziness, that was their only time alone. Had he found her note? Or was he retracting his offer altogether?

When their limo hadn't shown, Elaina's father ushered the wedding party onto a city bus, women first, as if they were escaping the *Titanic* instead of riding public transportation in formal wear, which meant once again she couldn't get close enough to Noah to have one simple conversation.

Officially, the reception didn't start until early evening. Unofficially, anyone who entered the restaurant would be fed and taken care of. All Jordan wanted was a break. And a few minutes alone with Noah at the very least.

Once inside the restaurant, she waited, anxiously watching guests pour in through the doors.

"Looking for someone?"

Griffin appeared at her side, a familiar face, but no. Not the one she was looking for.

"As a matter of fact I am," she said, then nodded toward the doorway where Maggie stood outside talking to Miles. "Maybe you can change her mind."

He sighed. "She told you about Washington?"

"Yep."

"And you don't think I've completely ruined everything?" he asked.

Jordan laughed. "I'm a hopeless romantic," she said. "I think if you guys love each other like I know you do, there's always a way to fix it."

She could believe that about other people. Easily. But was simply loving each other enough for her and Noah? Wouldn't he be with her now if it was?

Maggie stood just outside the glass door. Jordan and Griffin watched Miles kiss her on the cheek before disappearing down the sidewalk, but he didn't follow her inside. Jordan guessed he had other things to take care of, things involving a certain Greek chef, and this made her smile.

"You don't know where Noah went, do you?" she asked Griffin before she lost his attention completely.

"Not since he got off the bus. I'm sorry."

Jordan could feel his urgency to get to Maggie.

"Go," she said. "I'll be fine."

And that's all it took. Griffin left her side to make his way to Maggie's. Jordan took one last scan of the room and decided she wasn't quite ready to celebrate yet. As Griffin stepped outside to meet Maggie, Jordan offered a quick hello and slipped out the door.

It took her seven times to get the key card to work. *Seven.* Which was the perfect icing on a cake layered with frustration. Noah couldn't be bothered to answer his phone? Maybe send her a quick little text letting her know he hadn't been kidnapped and transplanted to some Greek isle where he was now in the hands of an evil yet beautiful island queen who he at first despised but after enough time with her learned to love?

Oh God. Her jet lag was making her delirious. She could pee, take a quick nap, and still make it to the *official* reception with time to spare.

Jordan tapped the light switch she knew was on the wall just inside the door, but nothing happened. In fact, for all the mid-afternoon sun, the hotel room was pitch black, as if there were no windows at all. *Great.* She'd have to feel her way along the furniture to make it to the bed lamp.

She kicked off her heels and shuffled along the floor.

"Ow. Dammit!"

Well, at least she found the nightstand. She bent to grab her throbbing toe, and after a couple of hops toppled butt-first, thankfully, onto the bed. When she flipped the lamp's switch, a warm glow illuminated the cave-like space, and the first thing she saw was a copy of E.M. Forster's *A Room with a View* next to the base of the lamp. No—it was *her* copy of the book, but she hadn't packed it, opting for her phone's e-reader app over a suitcase full of books.

"I don't…" Jordan ran her hand along the worn spine and finally took the object into her hands, knowing that somehow she was meant to look beyond the cover. Inside there was a Post-it, and on it only four words: *This isn't a proposal.*

Jordan laughed and then inhaled a hitching breath.

"Noah?" she whispered, half afraid he was going to jump out of a closet or something and make her pee her pants, but he didn't answer.

On instinct she scooted over to the other side of the bed and turned on *that* lamp. On the bedside table lay her copy of *Pride and Prejudice*. She opened to the title page, and on it she found another Post-it: *Because I already asked, and you said yes. Only men who are refused have to ask twice. *cough cough* Mr. Darcy *cough**

Jordan almost choked on the combination laugh/sob that tried to escape from her throat.

"*Noah,*" she pleaded. "Where *are* you?"

She heard the familiar buzz of her phone, alerting her to a text. She found her purse on the floor between the door and the bed, and she scrambled to read what she knew was from him: *Open the curtains.*

Jordan tried to run, but she was limping now, the toe-stubbing possibly a bigger issue than she'd originally thought, but there was no time to worry about injury when what she'd been looking for all day was hopefully on the balcony.

Drawing the curtains not only lit up the room, but it also lit up her heart. Because there stood Noah—jacket and tie gone but still in his button-down and kilt, a small velvet box in his open palm and a sprig of mistletoe held over his head. She could barely see through the blur of tears, but she was able to find the handle to the sliding balcony door and gave it a swift yank.

And the freaking thing didn't budge.

She watched Noah attempt to maintain his calm, but his eyes darted right and left, taking in the confines of the space. The *small* space. It may have been partially outdoors, but Jordan knew how Noah's mind played tricks on him if he got into a panic. In its altered state, Noah's brain could make him believe he was trapped even if he wasn't, and while she watched in horror waiting for him to cross that threshold, he began to laugh.

Great. He was already there, alone, and this was all her

fault. She would never forgive herself for ruining this trip for him, for ruining their engagement, and—were his lips moving?

Jordan swiped the back of her arm over her eyes and focused on Noah's voice because the door wasn't made of soundproof glass, after all.

"Brooks," he started, and she could still make out the laughter in his tone. "Unlock the door."

What? "How did you get out there if the door is locked?" she asked, though when she put her thumb and forefinger over the small latch and tugged it down, she felt the lock give way, and the door slid open with ease.

"This is us we're talking about. We do things the messy way. I've got the scar on my palm to prove it, and I seem to remember one on your forehead as well."

"It's possible I just broke my toe," she added, "but who's keeping score?" She took one hobbling step forward, and Noah shook his head.

His smile fell as he dropped the mistletoe and reached for her hand.

"Shit," he said. "The room was too dark."

He helped her back toward the bed and sat her down, kneeling to take her injured foot in his hand.

"How'd you know I'd come back to the room?" she asked.

He shrugged. "I didn't. After your note, though, I guess I bet on you wanting to find me. Good thing I was right or I'd have probably been out there until after the reception." He laughed quietly. "God, Brooks. I just wanted to give you the perfect proposal—a perfect memory to kind of, I don't know, replace the painful ones from the last time we were in Europe."

Her hands reached for his face, and she urged him up on the bed next to her.

"Is that what this is about? You think I regret anything

about the year we met?"

That little spot above his nose crinkled, and she wanted to kiss his adorable confusion away.

"Don't you?" he asked. "It's because of me we spent so much time apart that year."

She crossed her arms. This stubborn, wonderful man. When was he going to get it?

"Do *you* regret that year?"

He shook his head. "I met *you*."

"Then why would it be any different for me?" she asked, and he opened his mouth to say something, but she wasn't done. "Our road may have been a bumpy one, Noah. And maybe it still is from time to time. But it's *our* road. Do you get that? I can't regret anything that was on the path that led me to this moment—to the man I love wanting to spend the rest of his life with me."

She kissed his forehead. "*Nothing*, Noah. I regret *nothing*."

He let out a long sigh. It killed her to think that for three years he'd been carrying this with him, that he'd ever doubted how she felt about what she considered one of the best years of her life because it was the experience that brought her to him.

He pulled her legs over his, and he pushed up the narrow skirt of her dress so he could bend her knee. She winced when she saw the swollen pinkie toe on her left foot, but the heat of the pain turned to something else entirely when Noah pressed his lips to the top of her foot, then her ankle. Her calf. The bend of her knee.

"I'm sorry for making you think last night was anything other than our version of perfect," he said, lips still traveling farther up her thigh. "I love you." More kisses. "God, I love you."

"I love you, too. So much," she said, her head falling back onto the pillow. "I'm sorry for leaving."

He had already made it to the spot where her thigh and hip met, and Noah was getting dangerously close to rendering her speechless as he peppered kisses down the edge of her panties.

"I think," he started, kicking off his shoes, and then surprising her by sliding his thumb along that same border, lifting the lace away from her skin and allowing his tongue to startle her with a quick flick against her swollen center.

Jordan gasped, and he peeked up from between her legs, his eyes glinting with mischief.

"I think we can find a way to make it up to each other," he said, and then dipped his head again.

"Wait!" Jordan cried, and his head bobbed up, that adorable crinkle between his brows present once more. "The ring," she said. "*My* ring. If this isn't a proposal, we're already engaged, right?"

Noah's face broke into a smile, and he nodded while his other hand produced the small box. He popped it open with the flick of his thumb while his other thumb massaged the slick spot where his tongue had just been.

Jordan squirmed because, shit, she didn't want him to stop, but first things first.

She held out her left hand, and Noah dropped the box onto her belly, maneuvering the ring out with one hand so his other could stay otherwise occupied. As soon as the ring was back in its rightful place, Jordan fisted both her hands in Noah's hair, and he gave her one last grin before his face dropped out of view.

He wasted no time freeing Jordan of her underwear, spreading her wide to take his fill.

His tongue swirled around her outside while two fingers slid in, and Jordan bucked against the maddening pleasure, her heated belly coiled tight and ready to explode.

"God, Noah, I'm not going to last if you don't slow

down." She gasped with every word, and she wasn't sure she wanted him to ease up or bring her the fuck home, and then somewhere in her state she remembered that this gorgeous man between her legs was wearing a skirt, too.

"What's under the kilt?" she asked, and that stopped Noah in his tracks. He pushed himself up so his eyes met hers, his gaze heated like nothing she'd seen before. Sweat trickled between her breasts, and she was sure this dress was toast, but she was too far gone to care.

Noah unbuttoned his shirt and wriggled out of it so Jordan could feast on his lean, muscular torso—his runner's body—a sheen of sweat on his collarbone and chest. And then his hands went to work unfastening the kilt, and when it fell to the bed, Jordan had to swallow twice to make sure the saliva didn't pour from her lips. Because there was Noah, his full, beautiful erection unguarded and unsheathed.

"I figure you're only pretend-Scottish once, so might as well get into full character." He waggled his brows, and she almost came just at the sight of him.

She had no words, only gratitude that she was an organized woman, one who prided herself on routine, and in three years she'd never forgotten her pill, which meant she was ready for all the spontaneity she could handle.

She hooked her feet around his waist, and without saying anything at all, told him what she wanted—what she absolutely needed—because she knew he needed it, too.

He fell forward and tugged the zipper down the side of her dress, and Jordan dropped her legs so she could shimmy free of the garment.

"You're so beautiful."

"Tell me about it later," she said, and Noah barked out a laugh.

"Later it is." He pressed her knees so they fell open, and he rubbed his thumb up and down her wet folds, and Jordan was sure she would die of arousal if he didn't do something quick.

Then he lowered himself to her, giving her one small nudge with his tip before burying himself completely, and she cried out. He rocked inside her and slid his hands up the length of her arms, pinning them above her head.

His kisses were firm and relentless, and she couldn't get enough of him.

"How could you ever think we were anything but perfect?" Jordan asked, panting as if she were on her final breaths.

He slid out slowly, teasing her like the lovely, maddening, beautiful man he was.

The corner of his mouth quirked into a crooked grin. "My mistake," he said, and then rocked her until she called out his name…and promptly forgot her own.

Chapter Twenty-Nine

MAGGIE

Maggie meant to walk into the restaurant. It was as simple as putting one foot in front of the other, yet there she stood, holding her breath as Griffin approached. She'd shared an apartment with him for a year—shared her heart with him since the moment they'd met—yet he could still make her nervous, so much so that she couldn't decide if those were butterflies in her belly or just full-blown nausea. Not like he hadn't seen her lose her lunch before, though, right?

And there it was, the elephant in the room. She had survived a brain aneurysm but was forever changed, and she had learned to live with that—to accept this new version of herself. But Griffin had barely known her more than a year. He was still learning.

"Hey," he said, stepping outside the door and letting it fall closed behind him.

"Hey," she replied.

"Can we go somewhere and talk?" he asked, and God

how she wanted his easy smile instead of the hesitant one he gave her now, as if her answer determined whether or not that smile remained or fell completely.

"Back to the hotel?" she asked and immediately thought better of it. Things happened when she and Griffin were in a room alone together, and right now she wanted no distractions.

He must have read her afterthought, because when he said, "I just want to talk, Maggie," she let out a nervous laugh.

"I just don't want to get…distracted," she told him.

"I'm good at that?" he asked, and there was the smile, the one that melted her heart and sent a different kind of heat to other…parts.

"You know you are, so just shut up. We're supposed to be talking." But Maggie couldn't suppress her amusement.

Griffin took her hand, threading his fingers through hers, and the action was so unexpected, the touch of his skin so missed by her own, that she gasped.

"May I escort you back to our hotel, Ms. Kendall?"

He squeezed her hand, and the only response she could manage was to simply squeeze back.

Though the air was crisp, there was no breeze. Either the cardigan she had on over her dress was enough to keep her warm, or Griffin's heat pooled from his palm into hers, warming her from the inside out. She was pretty sure it was the latter, which would make letting go that much harder. And she had to let go. For Griffin to reach his full potential, she had to let *him* go.

But for the short walk down the brick-laid street, she pretended. Maggie dug into her small purse with her free hand, searching for her camera, but to capture the beauty of the old white buildings, the arched doorways, she'd need the hand that Griffin held, too. The longer she hid behind the camera, captured what was going on in other people's lives, the longer she could avoid what was happening in her own.

Wherever this conversation was headed, she wanted to avoid the destination for as long as possible.

"How about this?" he asked, slowing his pace until they were both stopped in front of a café where patrons sat under heaters at the outside tables. Griffin positioned her in front of him, wrapping his arms around her midsection, and Maggie couldn't help but lean into him. For balance, for warmth, for the sheer pleasure of just being near him, she pretended some more.

She focused on a brown pillar that extended from an ivory archway, pinpointing a spot where the paint had peeled away. *Click.*

The photograph slid out from the bottom of the camera like a serpent's tongue, and Maggie wasn't sure she could handle the sting the venom would leave. As the image came into focus, she let out a breath. It wasn't that she *needed* the camera like she used to, her short-term memory issues getting better each day. But when a moment presented itself, one she wanted to preserve for the long term, it was important to get it right.

The shot was wide, the small spot on the pillar in focus, but the swarm of people around it a colorful blur.

She dropped the camera back into her purse and handed Griffin the photograph before starting to walk again.

"This is really good, Pippi," he said, and her heart leapt just a little at the sound of his nickname for her. They would get through this talk, and then they could be Pippi and Fancy Pants for the remainder of the trip. Hell, they could pretend for eight more months if she wanted, but they had to lay it all on the table now before they could get through the rest.

"That's what Washington will be for you—a beautiful, amazing, chaotic blur."

"Maggie, don't…" he started, and she spun to face him.

"Don't what? Be realistic? Come on. This?" She motioned

between them. "This isn't a fantasy. It's *work*. That's why you didn't tell me about Washington, and that's why you're trying to convince yourself that you weren't seriously considering it in the first place because you know it will be the kind of work that you might not be cut out for—that *we* might not be cut out for. I get it, Griffin. I get it, and I don't blame you, and I'm not letting you say no to something you deserve…because of me."

"Maggie," he said again, but she wasn't going to let him argue against his own best interest.

"Look at where we are," she said, throwing her arms out wide and spinning around, her surroundings a blurred vision of pale concrete. "We are *missing* this because of *us*. I can't ask you to miss out on your future, too."

Griffin's jaw ticked, and his eyes darkened.

"Like you missed the wedding?" he asked.

"What?"

"The wedding," Griffin repeated. "Every second of every minute of every freaking *hour* we were apart today, I looked for you, but you weren't there. I know you're angry, but it isn't like you to bail."

Maggie plunged her hand into her purse and thrust a stack of mini Polaroids at him.

"Here's how much I bailed," she said, smacking the pile against his chest. She waited for him to look at the photos, for his eyes to widen.

"Maggie—" he started, but she interrupted him by shaking her head.

"I'm going to walk the rest of the way on my own, okay?"

What was happening with them? After everything, how could he think she'd bail on him? She set off alone, making it to the hotel in what felt like the space of a few labored breaths, the rest of the walk a blur.

Once inside the room, she pressed the door shut and

whacked her head against it. Shit. That was sure to be the express lane to a headache. Then came the pacing, and after that the mumbling to herself.

"Bailed? I can't believe he would think I was capable of missing anything this important. No matter what's going on with us, I would never miss out on such a big part of his life. *Bailed.*"

She groaned.

"Are you through?"

Maggie jumped and spun toward the door where Griffin leaned against it, arms crossed.

Her mouth fell open, but of course now the words wouldn't come.

Griffin took a step toward her, and she held her ground. Another step, close enough for her to smell the apple scent of the shampoo they now shared.

"Being apart from you last night was hell," he said, and although she was standing firm, all Maggie could do was nod. Because yes, it *was* hell.

There had been nights she'd come home to a sleeping Griffin and woken to an empty bed, him already gone for work while she slept in before a late class. There was that long weekend she went to Florida to visit her gran while Griffin was swamped with a project and had to stay back in Minneapolis. And she had missed him. But the light at the end of the tunnel was that they'd be back together.

But last night? Last night felt like the beginning of the end of…*something*. And that, Maggie realized, was her hell. The possibility of a life without Griffin.

"This one is my favorite," he said, handing her back one of the photos. She remembered sneaking out of the pew to get this shot, one where she had to squat to get the right angle to capture Griffin in his jacket and kilt behind the groom as the priest recited the wedding prayers. She'd been so focused on making sure she could see him from head to toe that she'd missed his expression—or the change in it.

"You were smiling when I set up the shot," she said. "Smiling and watching Duncan and Elaina, but you aren't even looking at them here."

Griffin shook his head.

"I was looking for *you*," he said.

"I didn't bail," she told him.

"I know." He let out a long breath. "And I'm not bailing on you, either."

Maggie held the photo against her chest. She'd had such a great argument prepared for this moment, and she was summoning the words to explain why he had to go, but Griffin never gave her a chance.

"What if I came down with the flu, right here and now?" he asked, and just as Maggie thought she was going to turn into a puddle of tears, she laughed.

"What are you talking about?" she asked.

"What if we get home, and I slip on some black ice and break my leg?"

"I know what you're doing," she said. "It's not the same."

He cocked a brow. "Answer the question, Pippi. If something happened to me, what would you do?"

She rolled her eyes. "I'd take care of you."

The corners of his mouth turned up.

"And if I *did* break my leg because I fell on black ice, how would you feel about my taking a leisurely winter stroll after I was healed?"

She grabbed his hand and slapped the photograph into his palm.

"This isn't fair," she told him. "All of these *what if*s aren't fair. You know going in, that if I come with you, you're going to spend energy worrying about me that could be better spent on your new job."

Again he stepped closer, and she had nowhere left to go but against the wall behind her.

"Maggie, I'm going to worry about you whether you are in D.C. or Minneapolis, whether you are in the bed next to me or in another apartment hundreds of miles away. Don't you get it? I *love* you. Above any other person or city or job—*you* matter most. Maybe I was scared to tell you the truth, and you're right. I shouldn't have kept any of it from you, and I'm a shit for doing that."

His palms were on her cheeks now. He was dangerously close to distracting her, and she had to stay focused.

"I was scared," Griffin said, and she closed her eyes and nodded. She knew fear all too well, knew that she was letting it take the lead with her as much as Griffin had let it with him. "And I'm still scared now—terrified, actually. But not for the reason you think."

At this her eyes fluttered open, and Griffin's gaze held her there, frozen in wait for what came next.

"Maggie, I'm not afraid of what will happen if you come with me to D.C. I'm scared of what will happen if you *don't*."

He kissed her then, and she couldn't do anything but kiss him back, this infuriating man who said all these things that made it impossible for her to stay mad at him.

"You're everything, Maggie. *Everything*. I may not have a ring to give you yet, but you have my heart. You have every part of me. It's not a choice—Washington or you." His lips found hers again, and then they were on her jaw, her neck, the lobe of her ear. "There *is* no Washington without you," he whispered against her. "I know it's not your dream and that you still have graduation, and if you decide it's too much…"

"I'll go with you!" she blurted, and then her hand flew to her mouth as if the sentence escaped her lips without permission.

"What?" Griffin's voice cracked on the word, and her

heart pretty much turned to goo.

"I'm going with you to Washington," she said, this time with conviction, and Griffin pulled back, his brows furrowing.

"I'd like to instate the WILD card," he said, "just to be sure," and Maggie bit her lip.

Ever since the night he'd won her over with a deck of UNO cards, the WILD card had always meant one of them got to ask a question and the other had to answer truthfully, no holds barred.

"Okay…" she said softly, and Griffin cleared his throat.

"Are you coming with me because I pushed too hard?" he asked, and Maggie shook her head.

"Are you coming with me out of guilt?"

"No."

"Are you coming with me because my legs look ridiculously sexy in a kilt?" He waggled his brows, and her expression broke into a smile.

"Are you planning on wearing the kilt in D.C.?" she asked.

"Not unless you require it." He was smiling with her now.

"Then no," she said. He opened his mouth again, but she pressed a finger to it. "I'm going with you because you're *everything*, Griffin. Because even though I'll always be afraid of the unknown, my future isn't tied to Minneapolis or Florida or Washington, D.C., or any one *place*." She ran a hand through his sandy waves, her palm resting on the back of his neck. "But it is tied to *you*."

He grinned. "And why is that?"

"Because I love you, Fancy Pants." Like he had to ask. She gave him a playful push.

"Hey…"

But she silenced him with a kiss, and Griffin pressed his whole body to hers as she parted her lips, and his tongue slipped past to tangle with hers.

In seconds, Maggie felt him firm against her, and her

brows shot into outer space.

"You're…you're *Irish*," she told him, and Griffin took a small step back.

"Aye, love," he said in an exaggerated brogue, eyes dark with need. "But for about eight more hours, I get to be a *true* Scotsman."

Maggie's eyes fell to Griffin's kilt, and she licked her lips, then swallowed, her throat suddenly dry as the desert. And Griffin Reed, Scottish for a day, was the only thing that could quench her thirst.

She pushed off the wall and closed the small distance between them, laying her palm over the part of the kilt where she'd felt him moments before. He sucked in a breath.

"You're not wearing one of those purse thingies," she said, and he shook his head.

"Pockets in the jacket," he said, his voice low and rough. "Plus, easier access for—" He sucked in a breath, losing his words completely as Maggie found the overlap in the tartan and slid her hand behind it, where she discovered the treasure she sought, her hand wrapping around his solid length.

"Easier access for whom?" she asked, and he let out a delicious groan.

"You, Pippi. Only and always you."

He dipped his head and kissed her—soft, sweet, expectant. But when her hand slid up his length, that sweetness turned to hunger, and Maggie's core burned with desire. She wasn't sure who needed whom more.

"Got anything interesting in those pockets?" she asked as he rocked into her palm and she stumbled back against the wall.

"Just for you, sweetheart." And Maggie's photographs rained onto the floor around them as he produced what she considered the best of the sights so far—a condom.

"Shit," he said. "Your photos, I'm sorry…"

But she had already grabbed and torn open the foil wrapper.

"I'm not worried about the moments that have already passed," she told him as she rolled the condom down his length. "I just want to enjoy the ones that are happening now."

Griffin gripped her thighs and slid her dress up over her hips. He hooked a finger under the hem of her panties and tugged, sliding them down her freckled thighs and to the floor, where she promptly stepped out of them. He was squatting now, and as he rose to meet her again, he placed a soft kiss between her legs, and Maggie let out a small cry.

"Where were we?" he asked once he was standing again. "Oh, that's right." He hiked her dress up again, and Maggie followed suit, raising the kilt to expose Griffin's erection. Then he lifted her onto him, and he sank inside her with ease, a perfect fit.

For the first time that day, Maggie was grateful for her toe-pinching heels. She hadn't anticipated this benefit, Griffin taking her up against a wall, but damn if these weren't going to be her favorite shoes from this day forward.

"Is this okay?" he asked, and she giggled that they were so in sync, not only physically but in their thoughts as well.

"Heels," she told him, and his lips parted in a smile against her.

"But is *this* okay?" he asked, and Maggie felt his hand leave her hip. Then it slid between them, Griffin's thumb swirling over her as he plunged deep into her core.

Her only response was a gasp as she felt her muscles tighten around him.

"Christ, Maggie," he hissed, and those were the last words he spoke as they tested the boundaries of this new position, of Maggie's balance and Griffin's persistence until finally, she rode him home.

Home. That's what it was all about, wasn't it? She got it

now, really got it, this whole loving-someone thing. It didn't matter where they were or what stage in their lives they were in.

"*You're* my home," she whispered as she clung to him on trembling legs.

Griffin kissed her…and kissed her…and though he had finished with her, it was as if he still couldn't get enough.

"And you're mine, Pippi. You'll always be mine."

Chapter Thirty

MILES

The official pre-dinner serving had begun. Waitstaff circled the main room of the restaurant, which had been transformed into a ballroom, tables and chairs wrapped in white, circling a small dance floor that at the moment stood empty.

Miles had just drained one champagne flute and was exchanging it for a new one when he felt a palm against the small of his back.

"I am off the clock for the rest of the evening." Alex's warm breath tickled the hairs on his neck. "Any suggestions on how I should spend my time?"

Another server approached, prompting Miles to treat glass number two like a shot of ouzo. He tipped his head back and swallowed the bubbling liquid in one long gulp. When the serving tray was in reach, he deposited his empty glass but was stopped short from snagging another as Alex's hand wrapped around his wrist. Finally Miles turned to face him.

"What's the rush?" Alex asked. "We at least have to make it until midnight."

Alex grinned, but Miles wasn't following.

"It's New Year's Eve, Miles. Who's going to finish the countdown with me if you consume a bottle of bubbly before dinner?"

Miles found another server coming from the opposite direction, and with his free hand he snagged his third drink.

"Cheers," he said, raising his glass. *I think I'd rather count flutes.*

This wasn't the truth. Miles wanted nothing more than to kiss Alex at midnight, but once that happened, he knew what came next. Good-bye. His heart-to-heart with Maggie and Jordan had buoyed him to action. He had let Alex in. But the closer they got to midnight, the closer they got to the one variable in the equation Miles couldn't work around—*good-bye.*

At least he sipped this glass. He could be civilized. After all, it was only five o'clock. To be drunk at a wedding before the sun had completely set? Well, Miles had *some* standards.

Alex crossed his arms and gave him the once-over.

"You do wear everything well, don't you?" Alex asked. "But this just needs a little…" And he reached for the knot on Miles's tie, maybe straightening it or maybe just looking for an excuse to make physical contact.

Alex himself wasn't wearing a tie, just a crisp white shirt under a tailored charcoal gray suit. He hadn't shaved, and Miles tried to ignore how the stubble on his jaw made him even more attractive. The look was effortless and at the same time made Alex seem as if he'd walked off the page of a fashion magazine. The bastard. This was why Miles needed more to drink. Maybe the champagne goggles would make Alex *less* attractive.

"Try this," Alex said, grabbing an hors d'oeuvre from a

passing waiter and bringing it to Miles's lips. Without thinking, Miles opened his mouth and let him drop the small puffed pastry on his tongue.

"It's just spanakopita, nothing too complex. But I do hear the chef has a secret ingredient that keeps the masses coming back for more."

His eyes fluttered closed as his teeth sank into the flaky crust to find the sautéed spinach and feta. Miles had bought the frozen version enough times to know the food, but he also believed Alex and his secret ingredient tease because everything this man made kept topping his list of best thing he ever tasted.

Note to self…more champagne will make his food less attractive, too, right?

"What's going on, Miles?"

Shit. He used to have the best poker face. Hell, his everyday face *was* his poker face. No one ever knew what was going on behind the ever-present grin. Maggie was the closest anyone ever got, but even she received the Miles Show every now and then.

"It's all good," he responded. "Good food, good drink, good-looking guy at my side…what more could I want?"

Alex rolled his eyes. "I don't know," he said. "Sounds like a pretty *good* night ahead of you, so why the whole asshole routine?"

Miles raised his brows, then took a sip of his champagne.

"That's just it. It's not a routine," he said. "This is the guy you should have met on the plane, so I'm introducing him to you now." He held his free hand out as if to shake. "Miles Parker. Nice to meet you."

But Alex didn't extend his hand.

"Jesus, Miles. You act like I asked you to move in or something. I asked for a weekend. A fucking *weekend*. And you're bailing after twenty-four hours."

He shrugged. "I'm leaving in the morning anyway. Why not get good-byes out of the way now?" As he said the words, Miles tasted the venom he spat in Alex's direction, and he hated himself for it. But this was best for both of them. An attachment had been formed, and they both had to know it. Miles was severing it before it became too much.

"You're absolutely right," Alex said, and his lips pressed into a thin line. "It was nice to meet you, Miles—at least the Miles I met yesterday. Say good-bye to him for me." He held up his glass and then drained the rest of it in a gulp. "And *you*," Alex continued, "you enjoy your last few hours alone."

And just like that, Alex walked away.

Miles nursed a Heineken now, the taste of champagne having soured. He was pretty sure he'd reached the topmost level of assholery he'd ever aspired to. But what was the point of prolonging the agony of leaving when he could leave now and drown said leaving at an open bar?

Elaina's father appeared in the center of the dance floor, his presence alone almost enough to silence the crowd. Miles crossed his fingers that he, too, would sport thick waves of salt and pepper when he was—what? Hosting his own daughter's wedding? He laughed under his breath, a bitter sound. It wasn't likely he'd be the kind of parent to grow old with his partner, contemplating empty nesting. He was more likely to be an empty nester for life.

Mr. Tripoli's broad build masked his slight paunch well enough. And shouldn't a chef boast a full belly? Ha! There was a strike against Alex—a body too perfect for that of someone you'd trust to prepare your food. Who trusted a chef who looked like he didn't eat his own creations?

Jesus, he was grasping now. Looking for fault and failing

miserably.

"Friends and loved ones," began Elaina's father in thick, accented English, his booming voice needing no microphone. "Please join me in welcoming my daughter, Elaina…and now my son, Duncan! Eat and drink, please. And celebrate! *Giortazo*!"

Guests halted where they were, glasses raised and faces painted with smiles, to watch the grand entrance of the newlyweds. But try as he might, Miles, for once, couldn't fake it. He raised his bottle, but the smile wouldn't come. Not when Elaina and Duncan walked in beaming; not when Jordan and Noah entered arm-in-arm, the light catching the engagement ring that had found its way back onto Jordan's finger; and certainly not after Thea walked in alone, her wedding party counterpart, Griffin, visibly missing from her side—only for him and Maggie to come running in at the last minute, Maggie's face a glowing giveaway as to why they were late.

The corners of his lips turned up, and Miles gave himself a mental pat on the back. He could still muster happiness for his friend despite what was certainly *not* envy at everyone's successful happy coupling.

The American contingent made its way to his table.

"Greetings," he said as Maggie pulled out the chair next to him. Griffin adjusted his kilt and took the seat on her other side. "Pink and green suits you, Mags."

Maggie's brows furrowed. "My dress is only green, Miles. Wait, did I spill something? I didn't eat any—" She backhanded him on the shoulder. "You're an asshole," she said, and Miles chuckled.

"Don't worry. No one other than Reed and me know you're freshly f—"

"Jesus, Parker," Griffin said. "Maybe you'd better slow down." He nodded to the bottle in Miles's hand. "And best friend or not, if I ever hear you say something like that to

Maggie again..."

Miles held up his hands in surrender. "You're right," he said. "Shit, Maggie. I'm sorry."

Noah and Jordan approached on Miles's right, and it was then that he noticed Jordan was limping.

He eyed the other happy couple. "Do I even want to ask?"

Jordan giggled as Noah helped her into her seat.

"Nope," she said, her smile permanently plastered to her face.

Miles slid his chair out and stood up.

"You know what, Reed? I think you're wrong. I think I'm going *too* slow."

He could make it through the night, but not if he had to sit in the middle of this...this circle of bliss.

He was barely to the bar when Maggie caught up with him, and he had to force himself to face her.

"Mags, I'm sorry. What I said—there was *no* excuse for that."

She skimmed her fingertips along his hairline and then cupped his cheek, the touch so full of love that his breath hitched.

"How did I get lucky enough not to scare you off?" he asked.

Maggie smacked his arm again.

"Hey! I deserved the one at the table," he said. "But what was that for?"

Maggie grabbed the almost empty Heineken from his hand and set it down on the bar.

"Because this isn't you, Miles Parker. I've never seen this guy before. You want to know why I love you so much?" She paused and waited for him to nod, which he did, accepting his scolding. Relishing it, actually. Someone needed to be a dick to him for how much of a dick he was to Alex.

Okay, so Maggie wasn't a dick, but she was lovingly pissed,

and that was close enough.

"I love you because you have the biggest heart. Because you're loyal. And because you helped teach me not to let my fear keep me from going after what I want." She paused again, but this time he could tell she wasn't waiting for anything from him. Her smile fell, and she started twirling a lock of her fiery hair. She was hesitating.

"Just say whatever you need to say, Mags. Nothing can sink me lower than I've already sunk."

She rolled her eyes. "Great," she said. "I'll just be the nail in the coffin of your shit day, then? Excellent."

He grabbed her hand and squeezed.

"Thought you had a grip on the fear," he said. "More than I do on the drama, I guess." He chuckled, and this seemed to encourage her.

"I'm leaving Minneapolis," she said, squeezing his hand back, and Miles's throat tightened.

"You're going to D.C. with Griffin."

She nodded, and he felt the ridiculous hot sting of tears. *Christ*, what was wrong with him? This was what he wanted for Maggie. This was what he told her she should do. But on some level he had hoped she wouldn't. Because Maggie staying would be a reason for him to stay—a reason for him to ignore what was missing from his life by focusing on someone else's.

"This is *good* news," he said, and he watched her swipe at a tear.

"Then why do you look so sad?" she asked, and he bit down hard on the inside of his cheek. Then he groaned.

"Because I'm a sad excuse for a human right now. Because if you didn't go with him, you'd end up like me. And as much as I'll miss you, I would never want that for you."

She wrapped him in a tight embrace, and he let out a shuddering breath as he squeezed her back. He knew when he let go that this would be the beginning of the end. Of all the people in his life, she was the closest thing to home. He'd been veering off course for years now. Without Maggie, he feared he'd be utterly lost. But that was not her burden to bear.

He pushed her from him, his hands firm on her shoulders.

"I'm *happy* for you, Mags. Do you get that? This is what I want for you."

She pulled him close again.

"I love you, Miles."

"I love you, too," he said.

He didn't want to know if she heard his voice crack on that pivotal word. It had been so easy to say it to her in the past. She was his closest friend, and he knew she would never leave. That was enough for him to hand over a little piece of his heart.

Little pieces could break, too. This wasn't what surprised him, though. What caught him off guard was the realization that he wouldn't have done it any differently. Things with Maggie would be different once she left. And yes, it would hurt like hell to say good-bye. But he would never give up the five years he spent letting her burrow into that tiny place in his heart. He wouldn't trade the hurt for never knowing her at all.

"Shit," he said.

Maggie pulled free of his embrace. "What?"

"Well, I'm twenty-six years old, and I think—maybe—I just fucking grew up."

Maggie laughed. "Is that a good thing or a bad thing?"

He shook his head, more at himself than anything.

"Would have been good if it happened before I royally fucked things up."

Her grin only grew wider.

"Miles Parker…" Her voice took on a teasing lilt. "Are you falling for a boy you met on a plane?"

He ran a hand through his hair. "That's crazy, right? I mean, not just the meeting-him-yesterday part. But he lives in *Greece*."

Maggie nodded. "I can see where that might make things difficult. What are your plans after earning that PhD this spring?"

"Maggie…"

"Do you have a job lined up? I know you wanted to teach. At a university. I hear they have those here."

He laughed. "I just basically told the guy to fuck off. I don't think he's asking me to move in anytime soon."

Maggie raised a brow. "But if you tell him how you feel and that you're all grown up now, and maybe bat those gorgeous baby blues, he might forgive you. You've got five months of school left. Who knows what could happen between now and then?"

He straightened his tie, then loosened it. Then he tore the fucking thing off.

"You're cute when you're falling for someone," she said.

"Shut up. I'm a fucking mess. Are you going to be okay if I go? I need to find Alex. Does this look okay without the tie? Jesus, my palms are sweating."

She stood on her toes and pecked him on the cheek.

"It's okay. You're actually adorable," she added.

She pulled her small camera from her purse and snapped a picture of him before he could object.

"Here," Maggie said. "So you remember the moment you decided to follow your heart."

Miles grabbed the photo and then took in a deep breath.

"So I'm doing this?" he asked, and even though she nodded, he didn't need her to answer. Maggie wasn't responsible for his happiness. And neither was Alex, for that matter. He still had a lot to learn about taking a chance on it, but he was the only one responsible for that.

He kissed the top of her head.

"I love you, Mags."

"Love you, too."

The image on the photo started to take shape as he began to walk.

He laughed hard when his form came into focus—a version of him he'd never seen before. A complete and utter mess.

He was tired of neat and pretty, of putting on a show. Alex just had to take a chance on the *real* him, the one who was done with the act. But Alex wasn't in the restaurant. Miles even snuck into the kitchen, but he knew what he'd find when he got there. No Alex. He was no longer on the clock, and it was New Year's Eve.

Alex could be anywhere.

Chapter Thirty-One

DUNCAN

How many people could they possibly know? Duncan had lost count four tables ago. And never mind the people who never sat down and just milled about. They didn't make the list. According to him, if you weren't seated you weren't greeted. Oh bloody well.

"One more," Elaina said. "And then we get to eat."

Duncan groaned until his eyes fell upon the familiar faces at this final table where they had to put on the bride and groom show. He collapsed in a chair next to Jordan, who sat with her feet resting on Noah's lap.

"You've got the right idea, Jordan." He watched Elaina dutifully kiss her American guests on each cheek, then patted his thigh with his palm. "Come sit, wife. I beg you. I can't stand anymore."

She obliged, sinking onto his lap and draping her arms around his neck. She kissed him, and he wished that when he opened his eyes, the party would be over and they would be alone in their hotel room bed.

No such luck.

"Do you know that's the first we've kissed without someone else asking us to do it?"

Sure, he'd been kissing her all night, but only on command when someone tapped a spoon against a glass or brandished a phone or a camera. This was the first kiss that was for no one else but them—and the four others at the table watching.

Elaina slipped her tongue past his lips, and bloody hell, Duncan couldn't give two shites that they weren't alone. She was his *wife*, and he would never refuse her lips on his.

When she did pull away, he felt light-headed, drunk even, and he hadn't had a single sip. He heard quiet laughter and finally opened his eyes.

"Maybe we should leave you two alone," Jordan said.

Duncan nodded. "Aye. Would it be inappropriate, though, to consummate the marriage at the table?"

Jordan was still giggling. "You do have easy access with the kilt."

Elaina raised a brow. "Not my husband. He wanted to be a gentleman instead of a true Scotsman. How would you say it? Oh, yes. Access denied."

Maggie joined in the laughter, and Duncan looked from Griffin to Noah, who were both eyeing each other and shrugging.

"No," Duncan said. "Please, lads. Tell me I didn't cover up just so you two could…"

Jordan had her hand on her belly, laughing so hard she began to hiccup.

"Duncan is the only man at this table wearing something under his kilt?" Elaina's smile was replaced with a set jaw and pursed lips. She stood. "Come. I need to speak to you alone."

Duncan didn't have to be told twice. He was standing in a fraction of a second. Food could wait a little longer.

"Better hurry," Jordan said. "It's almost midnight. You don't want to miss the countdown!"

"We will see you for breakfast, yes?" Elaina asked, but she didn't wait for an answer from any of them. Instead she stalked away from the table, Duncan's hand gripped firmly in hers, and she pulled him straight out of the restaurant.

She led him up the outside staircase, which led to the back apartment entrance. In seconds they were in her room, the one he came to this morning to make sure she would still agree to be his wife. And now here they were. Married.

"Take it off," she commanded, nudging the door closed with her beautiful arse.

"Wha'?" It wasn't as if his John Thomas wasn't standing at attention. But this was his wife's only wedding night, and he wanted everything to be just right.

"Take it off," she repeated. "The kilt. The fucking tartan knickers." She took a step toward him. "Take…" Another step. "It…" One more. "Off."

Elaina was close enough to touch, yet she seemed to have a few ounces of restraint left. Duncan's was quickly waning.

"What about the room? Didn't your cousins decorate it or something? I thought they're supposed to parade us off to our bridal bed."

He may have spent a bit too much time Googling Greek wedding customs.

"Shit, Duncan. I don't live in a small fishing village one hundred years ago." She paused for a moment. "Okay, if they are all drunk enough, they might parade us to the hotel, but that doesn't matter. You said it. We make our own luck."

He swallowed. "Aye. We do."

Her face broke into a magnificent grin.

"Then take it all off. Please. For me. For your wife."

He obeyed. For his wife. Aye. Anything for her.

He started with the jacket. The tie and shirt soon followed.

They could hear music below, but this wasn't a dance. No more performing. Just a man about to make love to his wife. Next came the sporran—not a *purse*—then the socks and shoes followed.

"Stop," Elaina said, but her voice had lost its authoritative tone. This was more of a plea.

Maybe he hadn't done too much research. Maybe this was Elaina realizing they should play by the book, follow tradition, and let the wedding guests pilot them off to the true marriage bed.

"I'm sorry," he said, and he reached for his shirt, but Elaina tugged it gently from his hand.

She pressed a palm to his chest, and then the other.

"I just want to look at you," she told him. "A minute to look at my beautiful husband."

He let out a shaky breath.

"Aye," he said, his voice a rough whisper. "Look."

She raked her fingers down his chest and up his back.

"And touch," she added.

He nodded. "Touch."

She kissed him, her tongue flicking out to tease his lips. Then she was sprinkling tiny kisses over his chin, his cheeks, and that damned bruised eye.

"Does it hurt?" she asked him.

He laughed. "Probably, but I can't concentrate on the pain when you're this close."

"Good."

She took a small step back, still facing him, and found the zipper on the side of her dress. She guided it down, and he saw her silky skin peek out from the parted fabric.

"Shite, Elaina," he growled, and this only made her smile.

The zipper was over her hip now, and Duncan practically choked as she stepped out of the dress and laid it over the footboard of the bed.

There stood his wife in nothing put a pair of strappy high-heeled shoes.

"Where are your knickers?" he asked, and she shrugged.

"I wanted to know what it would be like to be a true Scotsman."

Oh for fuck's sake. Duncan was done waiting. He wriggled out of his tartan briefs, his erection altering the way his kilt rested over his legs. Then he pulled her to him, kissing her with wild abandon as she pressed her body against his.

"Like this," he said, kissing her jaw, her neck, down to her breast before taking her firm peak into his mouth. "This is what a true Scotsman is like."

Elaina called out his name just as they heard the clamor below.

"Ten!" The countdown had begun, and Duncan felt a sense of urgency take over. He grabbed Elaina's hand and placed it on the belt of his kilt.

"Take it off," he said, echoing her own words at her. And she did. Then Elaina led him toward the bed, pushing him down on his back as she climbed over him and slid up his length.

"Nine! Eight! Seven!"

Bloody hell. After making love to his wife, Duncan wanted to snog whoever invented the oral contraceptive.

She teased herself with his tip, and he added women to the list. Whoever invented women was getting one hell of a snog after this.

He looked up at this beautiful woman who had promised to be his for the rest of her life, and he had to bite back something resembling a sob.

"I love you, Elaina McAllister."

She hummed. "Say it again. My name."

His back arched as she slid down and then up again.

"Elaina McAllister."

This time she let him push her open, and she sank over him, blanketing him in her warmth, and Duncan knew he was home.

"Duncan McAllister," she said as he swirled inside her.

"Aye."

"I love you, too."

Chapter Thirty-Two

GRIFFIN

"Ten!"

Griffin grabbed Maggie by the hand and pulled her from the dance floor.

"Where are we going?" she asked in a fit of laughter.

"Outside. I have a feeling about something."

So they ran out Ambrosia's front door.

NOAH

Noah pulled Jordan onto his lap.

"Nine!"

"I'm sorry I injured you with my *not a proposal*."

She stroked his cheek and ran her fingers through his hair.

"I wouldn't have it any other way."

"Eight!"

"Guess we wouldn't be us if there was no accidental

bodily harm involved."

He'd be full of scars by the time they were old and gray, and Noah chuckled despite the danger that lay ahead.

She kissed him on the cheek and smiled. "No. We wouldn't be us at all."

MILES

Guess the saying was right: you always found what you were looking for in the last place you looked.

Miles had walked the nearby streets for hours, the cobbled paths lit with bright lights as late-night revelers spilled out of clubs and cafés. He'd stood by the white tower as a horse-drawn carriage circled by carrying another pair of newlyweds. From the moment he stepped onto an airplane, people in love had surrounded him. And he'd had a shot at love himself.

But he'd blown it. So he wearily made his way back to Ambrosia. When he arrived he couldn't bring himself to go inside. Instead he slipped behind the restaurant, ready to ring in the New Year with nothing but the waves crashing against the shore.

Yet even in the brisk December air, he picked up the sulfurous scent of a recently struck match. Alex sat in the sand just in front of the outdoor patio, arms draped over his knees and a cigarette dangling from his lips.

"Those things will kill you," Miles said.

Alex laughed and bit down on the filter as he spoke. "So will a diet high in butter and cheese, but it's my livelihood."

"Thought it wasn't a habit," Miles added, lowering himself to the spot next to Alex.

"Told you," Alex responded. "Only when I need to clear my head."

"Baseball!" Miles blurted, and Alex narrowed his eyes.

Shit. His brain was moving faster than he could speak. "I played baseball—in college. I'm bisexual, and I played baseball, and I'm trying here, Alex. It scares the shit out of me, but I'm trying to give you more than a name—more than I've given anyone in years."

It was time to go big or go home, so Miles pulled the cigarette from Alex's lips and stubbed it out in the sand.

"I know what I want," Alex said. "What the hell do *you* want, Miles?"

He pressed Alex's forehead to his. "You," he admitted.

"Right. For the weekend."

Miles shook his head. "For as long as you'll have me."

There. He'd said it. It was out there.

But Alex sat quiet.

"Look," Miles said. "This makes zero sense. But I finish my PhD in May, and you travel, right? So...I don't know. Maybe we see where this goes."

Alex cupped the back of his neck with his palm.

"I want to trust you. I really do. But you're a mess."

Miles nodded. "I know. But that's the thing about meeting someone who makes you reevaluate the way you've been living your life. Kinda makes you want to clean up your shit."

"Seven!"

Alex sighed. "I was in New York to sign the final paperwork for my new position," he said. "Head chef. I wasn't going to tell you because I didn't think it mattered, but I'm moving to the States."

"Six!"

Miles felt a release in his chest, like the vise that had squeezed his heart so tight all these years had finally let go.

"Five! Four!"

"It matters," he said. "It matters."

Elaina

"*Three! Two! One!*"

      Elaina rolled onto her back, panting.

"Happy New Year," Duncan whispered and kissed her soft on the mouth. "Elaina McAllister."

God, she loved the sound of that name.

Maggie

Maggie shrieked with delight at the first sound of fireworks.

"I told you I had a feeling, Pippi."

She threw her arms around his neck and kissed him hard.

"All in," he whispered against her.

"All in," she said.

Noah

"You're really going to marry me, Brooks?"

      She tucked her head under his neck and squeezed him tight.

"Only if you promise to never stop calling me that."

Noah squeezed back.

"As you wish, Brooks. Happy New Year."

And then he kissed his fiancée with the broken toe and scarred eyebrow as he cupped her cheek with his equally scarred hand. Though they'd marked each other permanently, Jordan Brooks would never quite know the mark she left on Noah Keating's heart. But he'd spend the rest of his life trying to show her.

Miles

"We made it till midnight," Alex said, and Miles nodded, not wanting to do anything but kiss this man who could have written him off but didn't.

"We made it till midnight," Miles added.

Alex kissed him—long and slow, each touch of their lips a new possibility.

"Thank you for finding me," Alex told him.

"Thank you for wanting to be found," Miles said. "Happy New Year."

Epilogue

One Year Later

Elaina

Elaina stood in the bedroom doorway, peaceful as a picture, while Duncan ransacked the room. She rubbed her round belly, stifling a gasp at the onset of the next contraction. But even in the midst of his frenzy, her husband noticed, and he was at her side in an instant.

"How close?" he asked.

"Eight minutes. We still have time."

The hospital was a short ride from their apartment, so Elaina was sure they didn't have to leave yet. She let Duncan lead her to the rocking chair in the corner of the room, the one where just a couple of days from now, she'd nurse their first child.

She took in a deep breath, shaking as Duncan lowered her into the chair.

"Another one? Already? Shite. I'll find it, dammit. I'll find it."

She shook her head and grabbed his hand before he could pull away. The first tear trickled down her cheek, but Elaina's smile was unmistakable.

"The next time I sit here, it will be with our baby boy or girl."

Duncan dropped to his knees and hugged her tightly, planting sweet kisses all over her belly, the same thing he'd done when he found out they were pregnant. Though they'd both decided to throw caution to the wind after the honeymoon, discontinuing any form of birth control and seeing where that led them, Elaina hadn't anticipated things working so quickly. She laughed now when she remembered how scared she'd been to tell him.

With his head in her lap, Duncan shouted.

"Yes! Sweet mother of God, yes!" Then he scrambled on hands and knees, reaching under the dresser and pulling out the tartan scarf Elaina had worn on her wedding day. "I knew I put it somewhere safe after I washed it. Must have fallen behind the mirror."

He returned to her with the garment in hand and wrapped it over her shoulders—for her tonight and for the baby upon their return.

He reached for her hand once more.

"Are you ready to make our own luck, Mrs. McAllister?"

She winked at him. "Aye, Mr. McAllister." Then she swiped her thumb under his eye. "I thought you didn't like to cry." She teased him, yet seeing him like this squeezed her heart, a different kind of contraction. She definitely preferred this to what was happening in her midsection.

He shrugged. "Guess I'm not so afraid of what I feel anymore, not with you."

Elaina winced and sucked in a sharp breath. Another contraction.

"Okay," Duncan said, glancing at her belly. "Maybe I'm afraid of *that*." He squeezed her hand and grinned, and Elaina laughed through the pain. He helped her to her feet, guiding her toward the bedroom door.

And they left as two to return as three.

MAGGIE

Maggie rubbed the back of her neck as she tried again to get the key in the door. A migraine threatened to work its way up to that spot of blinding pain that would make this night unsalvageable. A quiet New Year's Eve was all she wanted. And coffee. Coffee would fix all.

The door swung open before she tried the key again, and Griffin stood before her, steaming mug in his hand.

"Tough day at the office?" he asked, and she let her art bag drop from her shoulder so she could first steal a kiss and then the coffee.

"They're great kids," she said. "And it was a great party, but I think they've zapped my last ounce of energy. I'm probably not going to be much fun tonight."

Griffin led her to their small living room, set her coffee on the side table, and let her collapse onto the couch. Lucky enough to find a job providing art therapy at a local youth center, Maggie kept hours that rivaled his.

"Smells good," she said, closing her eyes for just a short moment.

Griffin kissed her on the forehead, then escaped back into the kitchen.

"Pizza," he called back to her. "The kind with no preservatives."

She smiled and opened her eyes, the rest and caffeine sure to do the trick. That's when she saw the UNO box on the coffee table.

"Game night?" she asked, and Griffin popped his head out of the kitchen.

"Pizza needs ten more minutes. Figured you could shuffle and get it set up?"

Maggie shrugged. "You got it, Fancy Pants."

She grabbed the box and gasped, not prepared for its lack of weight. In fact, the box was practically empty except for whatever made the soft rattling noise inside.

She took a few deep breaths. Whatever was happening, she needed to focus—not on exhaustion or hunger or anything outside this moment. Because her eyes already stung, and her heart might burst from her rib cage. There were no cards in the box, and if the *whatever* that was happening was the *something* she suspected—oh my God.

With trembling hands, she opened it, and a small diamond ring fell into her palm. When she looked up, her vision blurred through tears, there was Griffin on his knee on the other side of the table.

"Pippi...I need to ask you something." He slapped the naked deck of cards down on the table.

She nodded, her whole body a virtual earthquake.

"I know the ring isn't much, but if you don't mind waiting, someday it will be more."

She wanted to tell him she didn't care about the size of the ring. She wanted to scream the word *yes* before any question was even asked, but she couldn't do anything other than nod and try to control the trembling.

"No matter where I go," he said, and she noticed the tremor in his voice, "*you* will always be my home. Tell me I can always be your home, too. Be my wife, Maggie."

Griffin slid the deck toward her.

"Full deck," he said. "All in...always."

She was on her knees now, crawling around the coffee

table to kneel in front of him. She raised a hand to his face and swiped away the tear that lay on his cheek. She was doing that nodding thing again, unable to find her voice, and Griffin started to laugh.

"Is that a yes?" he asked, taking the ring from her palm and sliding it onto her finger.

She laughed now, too. "Yes." She kissed him. "Yes." He kissed her back. "Yes."

JORDAN

Jordan looked from Noah, to Elvis, and back to Noah again. "You sure?" he asked. "Your family's going to be pissed."

She laughed and nodded.

"They don't have to know," she said. "This is just for us, right? We changed the date so Duncan and Elaina could make it. Technically, we'd have already been married by now."

He grabbed her hand and squeezed.

"I guess you can't argue with *technically*."

She beamed at him. "Nice outfit, by the way."

"You as well," he said.

Actually, they looked ridiculous, but that was part of the fun, right? Jordan in her blue sweatshirt that read GROOM and Noah in the white one that read BRIDE. After all, she needed her something new, borrowed, and blue. The old was the Aberdeen T-shirt she wore underneath, a reminder of where and how they began.

She had suggested the Vegas idea as a joke, but you know what they say. In every joke there is a sprinkling of truth, and *truth* be told, Jordan wanted to marry Noah Keating today—and again in the summer. So when she opened her Christmas card from him, one that read, "This might be another proposal," she'd tackled him to the floor with kisses and a resounding *YES.*

But this wedding would be just for them. Them and Elvis.

The musical trio began the first few bars of "Can't Help Falling in Love," their cue to make their way toward the man in the bedazzled white jumpsuit who would pronounce them husband and wife.

Jordan linked her arm in Noah's, and they took their first step. Together. And when she tripped on her shoelace, they promptly fell. Together.

"Quick check for injuries," Noah said. He patted himself down. "All clear."

Jordan rubbed the elbow that broke her fall but echoed his answer just the same. "All clear," she said. "It's a good sign, right?"

Noah kissed her and then helped her up.

"I'd be worried if this went off without a hitch," he said and chuckled. "Now I'm sure we're making the right decision."

Jordan swatted him on the shoulder. "You weren't sure before?"

He grabbed her hand and threaded his fingers through hers.

"Eyes on the polyester, Brooks."

They took another step. She nodded.

"Eyes on the polyester."

They weren't Beatrice and Benedick or Lizzie and Darcy or Lucy and George. They weren't anything like the stories she'd read and loved for so many years. They were Brooks and Noah, and their tale was still just beginning. But Jordan knew, even before getting to the end—this would be her favorite story of all.

Miles

"Good night, Professor Parker. Do remember it's a holiday."

"Good night," he echoed, then hit the *end* button on his phone. On the one hand, Miles was thrilled to hear from Professor Norton, the head of the psychology department. They'd be taking him on full-time next year. On the other hand, it was nine thirty on New Year's Eve, and he was in his office with nothing but twenty-two ungraded term papers to celebrate with.

A soft knock sounded on the door, and he groaned. Miles thought he was the only one in the building. God, what if it was one of his no-shows from his office hours before the holiday break? That's just what he wanted to do, argue grades with some irresponsible freshman who couldn't be bothered to keep an appointment.

He pushed himself up from his chair and rubbed at his burning eyes.

"No office hours without an appoint—" he started, but when he opened the door, he found no student waiting for him. Instead, there stood Alex with a large shopping bag. Steam rose from the top of said bag, and Miles salivated at the escaping aroma. Lemon, garlic, spinach—he could feel the flakes of phyllo dough melting on his tongue.

"I thought you were working tonight."

Then again, Miles couldn't keep their schedules straight. As a first-year adjunct at NYU, he'd earned the shittiest schedule along with the shittiest office. But he was a professor of psychology at a university. And that? That wasn't shitty at all.

Alex backed him inside. "I am," he said. "Taking care of the deliveries tonight."

Miles fell back into one of the two student chairs in front

of his desk, and Alex took the one next to him, promptly emptying the bag onto a spot he cleared for the goods.

Miles blinked and scrubbed a hand over his jaw. "But you don't do deliveries."

Alex stopped what he was doing and grabbed him by the collar of his shirt, kissing him until all the other questions melted away.

"I *missed* you," he whispered against him. "So I snuck away for an hour. I've got everything under control."

Miles sunk back into his chair and let out a sigh. Alex had worked Christmas Eve and Christmas Day. He'd worked nearly every holiday since Miles had moved to New York in June. But somehow they were making it work.

Alex opened a container of egg lemon soup and handed it to Miles with a spoon. He grabbed it greedily, finally aware of his hunger.

"Where's my spanakopita?" he asked, the spoon still in his mouth.

Alex laughed and opened another container. "So demanding."

It was moments like these that made it work. And Alex crawling into his bed each night, his arms wrapped around Miles each morning.

Moments like this—and food—and trust. Miles was still new to that last one, but it was growing on him every day.

"Happy New Year, Miles," Alex said and kissed him again.

The happiest, Miles thought.

Alex pinched another of his savory pastries between his fingers and held it to Miles's lips. "More?" he asked.

Miles smiled and licked his kiss-swollen lips.

"Don't mind if I do."

Acknowledgments

Thank you to my agent, Courtney Miller-Callihan. I told you I wanted to write an ensemble romance from seven different points of view, and you believed that I could pull it off. To my amazing editor, Karen Grove, you had enough faith to let me try this crazy idea, and then you helped make it all pretty and sparkly. I'm so grateful to get to work with you.

My books wouldn't happen without my wonderful critique partners. Natalie Blitt, Megan Erickson, Lia Riley, and Jennifer Blackwood, you all complete me. Also, Miles and Alex especially appreciate your help in their scenes.

To my family, thank you for your undying patience and support. S and C, thank you for your wide-eyed excitement every time you see a book with Mommy's name on it. I love you times infinity.

Thank you to all the wonderful readers who fell in love with Jordan, Noah, Elaina, Duncan, Griffin, Maggie, and Miles in *If Only* and *What If*. Your emails and messages mean the world. So many of you asked if there would be a wedding in Greece, and I'm thrilled to say the answer is yes. Here it is. I hope you enjoy.

About the Author

A.J. Pine writes stories to break readers' hearts, but don't worry—she'll mend them with a happily-ever-after. As an English teacher and a librarian, A.J. has always surrounded herself with books. All her favorites have one big commonality—romance. Naturally, her books have the same. When she's not writing, she's reading. Then there's online shopping (everything from groceries to shoes) and a tiny bit of TV, where she nourishes her undying love of vampires and superheroes. And in the midst of all of this, you'll also find her hanging with her family in the Chicago 'burbs.

Connect with A.J. Pine and find out more about upcoming books at AJPine.com.

Discover the **If Only** *series…*

IF ONLY

WHAT IF

www.ingramcontent.com/pod-product-compliance
Lightning Source LLC
Chambersburg PA
CBHW031952240626
47153CB00003B/954